The MIT Press   Cambridge, Massachusetts   London, England

introduced, translated,
and with drawings by
JOHN A. STUART

THE GRAY CLOTH

PAUL SCHEERBART'S

NOVEL ON

GLASS ARCHITECTURE

This book was set in Geometric 415 by Graphic Composition, Inc., Athens, Georgia, and was printed and bound in the United States of America.

Library of Congress Cataloging-in-Publication Data

Scheerbart, Paul, 1863–1915.
    [Graues Tuch und zehn Prozent weiss. English]
    The gray cloth : Paul Scheerbart's novel on glass architecture /
introduced, translated, and with drawings by John A. Stuart.
       p. cm.
Includes bibliographical references.
ISBN 0-262-19460-0 (alk. paper)
  1. Scheerbart, Paul, 1863–1915. Graues Tuch und zehn Prozent weiss.
2. Architecture in literature.   I. Stuart, John A. II. Title
PT2638.E4 S3413 2001
833'.912—dc21
                                  2001030330

For Joel

CONTENTS

ACKNOWLEDGMENTS

Many institutions and individuals have generously supported this proj-
ect. My work in archives in the United States and abroad was spon-
sored in part by a 1995 National Endowment for the Humanities
Summer Stipend, a 1997 grant from the Graham Foundation for
Advanced Studies in the Fine Arts, and a 1998 fellowship from The
Wolfsonian–Florida International University (FIU). In addition, the FIU

Acknowledgments

Department of Sponsored Research and Training and the FIU School of Architecture have provided critical publication assistance. Several key individuals have kindly facilitated my work: Mary McLeod followed the project as it grew out of a paper in her Gender and Architecture seminar at Columbia University's Graduate School of Architecture, Planning and Preservation. Joan Ockman helped me focus my thoughts during graduate work at Columbia and beyond. And Rosemarie Haag Bletter of the City University of New York Graduate Center has unfailingly encouraged my research and offered expertise gleaned from her exceptional dissertation and seminal articles on the subject. Eric and Kati Dluhosch have been constant sources of intellectual stimulation, encouragement, and friendship during their winters in Miami. Kenneth Frampton, Zaha Hadid, Michael Sorkin, and the late Wayne Berg, each in their own way, provided the inspiration and guidance to engage architecture simultaneously through drawing, research, and writing. In Berlin, very special thanks are due to my good friend Laurie Stein, Curator of the Deutsche Werkbund Archiv; Angelika Thiekötter, Director of the Deutsche Werkbund Archiv; Magdalena Droste, then Director of the Bauhaus Archiv; Michael Matthias Schardt; architectural historian Despina Stratigakos; and especially to Mechthild Rausch, a leading expert on Paul Scheerbart, for her exceeding generosity. At Florida International University, time, funding, and other resources were contributed by William G. McMinn, FAIA, Dean of the School of Architecture; Dr. Thomas A. Breslin, Vice President for Research and Graduate Studies; Catherine F. Thurman, Director of Sponsored Research; Sonia O. Cabrera, Grants Special Supervisor; Cathy Leff, Director, Pedro Figueredo and Francis Xavier Luca, librarians, and other staff at The Wolfsonian–FIU; and Douglas F. Hasty and Ana Arteaga in Interlibrary Loan. Many colleagues and friends have provided invaluable encouragement and knowledge, sometimes in ways difficult to express. They include Adolfo Albaisa

Acknowledgments

and Kristopher Musumano, Elizabeth Alford, Lucia Antonelli, Ted Baker, Sunil Bald and Yolande Daniels, Juan Antonio Bueno, Claudia Busch and Gustavo Berenblum, Margaret Crawford, Catherine Croft, Edward Dimendberg, Edward and Sarah Eigen, Diane Ghirardo, Ethel Goodstein, Alison E. Isenberg, Sandy Isenstadt, Mark Jarzombek, Wendy Kaplan, Ariela Katz, Pat Kirkham, David Lewis, Rose-Carol Washton Long, Iraj Majzub, Nicolas Quintana, Erika D. Rappaport, John F. Stack, Jr., Katharine Howe Toledano and Macon Toledano, Henry Urbach and Stephen Hartman, Iain Boyd Whyte, and Mary Woods. And special thanks go to Roger Conover at the MIT Press, who provided the vision and motivation to complete this work, to Anne Marie Oliver and Matthew Abbate for their skillful editing of the manuscript, and to Jean Wilcox for her masterful book design. Several people, however, are at the heart of this project, including Wayne and Joanne Stuart, Megan Aimore, Todd Stuart, Allegra Stuart, and Ann and Bernard Hoffman, for their love and belief in my abilities; the wonderful and talented Evamaria "Mutti" Stolz, who painstakingly proofread the translation and who, along with the late Albert Stolz, Friederike Stolz, Tilmann Stolz, and Tine and Hugo Duchemin, invited me into their lives at a difficult time and patiently taught me German over the years; and the marvelously gifted Joel Hoffman, for his continuous editing, feedback, and loving companionship. To all of these people, I owe my humblest thanks.

INTRODUCTION

Fiction and Architecture

You absolutely must read Paul Scheerbarth
[sic] . . . in [his] works you will find much
wisdom and beauty.

WALTER GROPIUS TO HERMANN FINSTERLIN,
APRIL 17, 1919[1]

It is difficult to exaggerate the relationship between fiction and architecture. While nonfiction is often privileged as a "factual" source of cultural and political values, fictional narratives and architectural interventions also reflect deeply held hopes and ambitions. The line between fact and fiction is often unclear. Examples of architectural environments that demonstrate this porous boundary include computer simulations and virtual spaces, theme parks and world expositions, and many development strategies. All architecture must, in some sense, be imagined before it can be constructed, and literary and filmic fictions frequently expand upon or challenge perceptions of space and society. Notably, Ayn Rand's *Fountainhead* (1943) weaves a tale of capitalism and architectural heroism drawn from Frank Lloyd Wright's impact on midcentury America, as Le Corbusier, Wallace K. Harrison, and others were embroiled in forming a consensus over the design of the United Nations. Such diverse works as William Morris's novel of life in twenty-third-century London, *News from Nowhere* (1890); Ridley Scott's *Blade Runner* (1982), a fantasy of Los Angeles in 2019; and Peter Weir's *Truman Show* (1998), set in contemporary Seaside, Florida, invoke fiction to ask important questions of contemporary built environments and the politics that shape them.

Paul Scheerbart's 1914 *The Gray Cloth and Ten Percent White: A Ladies Novel* should be considered within this context.[2] Like *Blade Runner*, Scheerbart's novel peers into a world some forty years ahead of its time. Scheerbart utilizes this marginal future—more than a generation away, yet close enough to fall within a lifetime—to engage real and fictional conditions in a narrative that enhances our understanding of both. Swiss archaeologist-turned-architect and newlywed Edgar Krug, the novel's protagonist, circumnavigates the globe by airship with his wife, Clara. Krug populates the planet with wildly varied, colored-glass buildings, including an elaborate high-rise and exhibition/concert hall in Chicago, a retirement complex for air chauffeurs on the Fiji Islands, an elevated-train structure traversing a zoological park in northern India, a suspended residential villa on the Kuria Muria Islands, and a museum of ancient "Oriental" weapons on Malta. Surprisingly, Krug fears that his idiosyncratic but popular architecture is challenged by one significant component of environmental design: women's clothing. In response to this perceived provocation, Krug insists that his wife agree to wear all gray clothing with a prescribed addition of ten percent white. This odd sartorial dictum renders Krug notorious in the press, sensationalizes his international building campaign, and provides the title of the novel, thereby implicating readers in the confluence of architecture with fashion, gender, and global media.

 The Gray Cloth is the culmination of Paul Scheerbart's prolific literary career. Scheerbart (1863–1915) was a German architectural visionary, author, inventor, and artist engaged in the avant-garde circles of his day. He wrote dozens of fictional utopian narratives related to glass architecture. In *The Gray Cloth*, never before translated into English, Scheerbart employs a masterfully complex and subtle irony to disseminate theories on colored glass previously outlined in *Glass Architecture*, his well-known treatise of the same year. *The Gray Cloth* reverberates with the magical simplicity of a German fairy tale. Along with younger contemporaries, such as Bruno Taut, Walter Gropius, and Ludwig Mies van der Rohe, Scheerbart sought a modern language to critique a world transformed by global technologies, international politics, and the culture of abstract art. In *The Gray Cloth*, he weaves delicate and detailed descriptions of the colored-glass architecture he so eagerly anticipated, while addressing the star system in architecture and related issues of media and image in Europe and America. Scheerbart's minimal narrative, constructed of brief scenes

Benjamin

and aphoristic phrases, reveals perhaps more through what is absent than what is stated. Scheerbart's contribution of direct and precise language to German literary modernism led Walter Benjamin to comment that Bertoldt Brecht had ended "what Scheerbart had best begun."[3]

In many ways, *The Gray Cloth* is a response to and critical commentary on Germany's development in the first decade of the twentieth century. Germany experienced unprecedented economic growth and established a policy of *Weltpolitik* that promoted imperialistic expansion through its enhanced naval forces. Around the world, German goods were in greater demand than ever before. Desires to improve Germany's national design image led to the establishment of the German Werkbund in Munich in 1907. The Werkbund was intended as a union of artists and businesses dedicated to promoting German technology and design in global markets. In the summer of 1914, the first international exhibition of the German Werkbund opened, revealing to Europe and the rest of the world the results of nearly seven years of programmatic efforts to unify craft and industry to produce high-quality design. Supporters of artistic individualism in architectural design produced several of the most celebrated buildings in the exhibition. These included the office and factory building of Walter Gropius and Adolf Meyer, the flowing Werkbund Theater by Henry van de Velde, and the crystalline dome of the Glass House of Bruno Taut (to whom Scheerbart dedicated his manifesto *Glass Architecture*).[4] The outbreak of World War I on the first of August caused the abrupt closing of the Werkbund Exhibition. Fourteen months later, Paul Scheerbart died during the long war that he often feared would destroy Europe.[5] Though *The Gray Cloth* offered trenchant social commentary and held the potential for dynamic impact within the architectural community, this was obscured by the timing of its publication.

Paul Scheerbart and the History of Architecture

Paul Scheerbart was born on August 1, 1863, the eleventh and last child of Carl Eduard Scheerbart, a Pole, and Friederike Scheerbart, a Prussian, in what was then the west Prussian city of Danzig (now Gdansk, Poland).[6] Scheerbart's mother died when he was four, his father when he was ten, and all of his siblings before his sixteenth birthday.[7] At the age of twenty-two, Scheerbart moved permanently to Berlin to earn his living as a journalist.[8] Although many details of his early career are vague—Scheerbart, like others, fictionalized his own autobiography—the author became a culture and arts writer for the little-known *Berliner Börsen Courier*. In 1892, striving to find a readership for his work, Scheerbart formed Die Verlag Deutscher Phantasten (The publishing house of German fantasists). He had also become a regular participant in the Berlin literary café gathering or *Stammtisch* held at and named after a pub called Das Schwarze Ferkel (The black piglet).[9] There he encountered several of the most influential Berlin writers and critics of his time, including Julius Hart (1859–1930), a writer notable for introducing naturalism into modern German literature; Richard Dehmel (1863–1920), a poet known for promoting unfettered individualism and passion; and Stanisław Przybyszewski (1868–1927), an essayist and playwright considered the father of modernism in Polish literature. Scheerbart wrote about glass architecture for over twenty years, and in 1910 he started working with Herwarth Walden (1878–1941), the avant-garde publisher and promoter of expressionism. Scheerbart's first contact with the publisher occurred in 1904, by which time Walden had already served as the editor of several arts and critical journals, including *Morgen* (Morning or Tomorrow) and *Das Theater*. In 1910 he founded the progressive art and literature journal *Der Sturm*, in which Scheerbart published more than twenty articles.[10] Walden and his wife Else Lasker-Schüler (a German lyric poet and writer), Scheerbart and his wife Anna, and their friend Salomo Friedlaender (a philosopher and critic) formed the core of a prominent *Stammtisch* at the famous Berlin Café des Westens.[11]

During the most productive years of his life, between 1910 and 1915, Scheerbart lived in Berlin-Lichterfeld, a southwest suburb and the location of his beloved Palm House in the Berlin Botanical Gardens. Lamenting this building's lack of color and its wasteful, uninsulated glass walls, the author still admired the Palm House's power to unite glass architecture with nature in a constructed landscape.[12] While he was living in Berlin-Lichterfeld, Scheerbart suffered from numerous ailments in his legs and rarely strayed from this suburban setting. When he died from what may have been a stroke on October 10, 1915, Anna Scheerbart faced utter poverty. She sold what remained of his literary estate in bits and pieces, thereby fragmenting the history of these documents forever.

Between 1889 and 1915, Scheerbart published nearly thirty works ranging from novels and theater pieces to his more technical treatises, including *The Perpetual Motion Machine* (1910) and *Glass Architecture* (1914), as well as hundreds of articles for newspapers, magazines, and anthologies. Throughout his literary career, Scheerbart strove to integrate his spiritual and romantic leanings with the modern world, often relying on glass architecture to achieve this. In 1904 he wrote:

The frantic exertion I have nevertheless made to forge a connection between this era of socialism, technology, and militarism and my amazing and very religious life, absorbs my so-called human life. It is the source of my books, which always attempt to unite what is difficult to unite—to move a desiccated period driven by quantity slowly toward a "new" romanticism and a "new" piety.[13]

Glass Architecture, Scheerbart's best-known work, may be considered (along with *The Gray Cloth* and *Lesabéndio*) his most important attempt to forge such connections. The expository *Glass Architecture* provides striking similarities and contrasts to Scheerbart's fictional output. The work outlines his ideas in 111 chapters, each roughly composed around a single theme, presenting his ideological and technical interests without the veil of humor and irony usually found in his fictional works. Scheerbart correctly envisioned that *Glass Architecture*, like most of his writings, would serve several purposes simultaneously. While supplying practical recommendations for constructing domestic space without brick, wood, or mirror, Scheerbart expressed his conviction that the widespread use of colored glass would transform civilization spiritually and globally.[14] The author refused to consider this transformation "utopian," stressing the existence of building technologies already in place to facilitate change.[15] Scheerbart praised engineers and called for a new architecture to evolve from existing technologies. In this regard, he formulated a position aligned with that of Hermann Muthesius, the founding leader of the German Werkbund. Although there is no evidence of a dialogue between the two, they shared a vision for the ideological if not aesthetic path of modern architecture. In 1902, Muthesius elucidated his stance on the potential of glass and steel in *Style-Architecture and Building-Art: Transformations of Architecture in the Nineteenth Century and Its Present Condition:*

In these works [of engineers] a completely new and modern cultural spirit speaks, one which, as undeveloped as it may be, is born out of the most characteristic needs of our time and—far more than the efforts of architects that emanate all too much from the imitation of styles—must be termed its genuine offspring.[16]

Muthesius also shared Scheerbart's interest in color, specifically its connections with nature and its use in women's fashion design. Evidence of this may be found in his design of the Farbeschau, a pavilion on the theme of color, at the 1914 German Werkbund Exhibition in Cologne.[17] Behind its dowdy classical facade, the pavilion educated visitors on the history and practical use of color through displays of semiprecious stones, butterflies, birds, and flowers. According to contemporary accounts, the pavilion's greatest spectacle was a wide room illuminated by electric lights, which featured fashion shows with the latest creations in German, as opposed to French, evening wear. Far from the kaleidoscopic treatment of color in both Taut's Glass House and Scheerbart's descriptions of glass architecture, Muthesius exhibited *Echtfarben* (true colors) whose tones and hues, it was thought, were immutable under any light source.[18]

Muthesius's interest in "true colors" was part of a broader search for a *sachlich*, or "straightforward," approach to design that rejected ornament of any kind. From the outset of his career, Scheerbart was, on the contrary, interested in building ornamentation and its potential to create polychromatic urban environments. In *Glass Architecture* he called on readers to "resist most vehemently the undecorated 'functional style,' for it is unartistic." Unornamented architecture, according to Scheerbart, should be accepted only as a "transitional style" that eliminated "imitations of older styles."[19]

Glass Architecture was to be frequently read not only by the German expressionists shortly after World War I but by architects and architecture critics well into the 1920s and 1930s. Despite its eventual popularity, the manuscript was rejected by Scheerbart's literary publisher, Georg Müller, a fact the author noted with consternation in a letter to his friend Richard Dehmel in early 1914: "[My] book 'Glass Architecture,' which I assumed he would certainly take, was rejected after eight weeks in storage, at which time he maintained that the reader would not find it to be literature, but rather 'practical building suggestions!' Oh, sure!"[20] Scheerbart's own perception of *Glass Architecture* as a direct continuation of the utopian ideals he had explored in earlier narratives is clear both from his choice of a literary publisher and his response to that publisher's critique. Walter Benjamin, likewise, considered Scheerbart's manifesto, ultimately published by Herwarth Walden, within the context of his narrative work and concluded that the former presented social constructions associated with the development of glass architecture "in utopian contexts."[21] In the past forty years, however, discussion of Scheerbart has largely focused on the reinsertion of *Glass Architecture* into the history of functionalism, for what Reyner Banham perceived as its "sharp sense of the practicalities of using the new material."[22]

Several opportunities for technical writing came to Scheerbart through his collaboration with Bruno Taut on the Glass House at the Cologne Werkbund Exhibition. The novelist considered this commission "the greatest event of my life."[23] Scheerbart contributed maxims on glass and color to be engraved on the entablature of Taut's Glass House and wrote at least one description of the pavilion in which he outlined the potential for glass and concrete construction. Taut dedicated the Glass House to Scheerbart who, in turn, dedicated *Glass Architecture* to Taut. Scheerbart had met Taut through his efforts to form a "Society of Glass Architecture" near the end of his life. In July 1913, Scheerbart wrote to Gottfried Heinersdorf, the son of an old acquaintance and principal of the glass manufacturing and design company Puhl und Wagner, Heinersdorf, to ask for assistance in the creation of such a group.[24] At that time Heinersdorf's firm had formed a collaboration with Bruno Taut on the Cologne pavilion.[25] Although Scheerbart and Heinersdorf were distant acquaintances, the glass manufacturer quickly introduced the author to Taut.[26] Less than two weeks later, Scheerbart thanked Heinersdorf, stating that he was ready to meet "the glass architect."[27] Already by the end of 1913, while the Glass House was still being designed, Scheerbart used familiar German to address the young Bruno Taut, thanking him for his gift of a small book on China and keeping the architect updated on the progress of *Glass Architecture* and *The Gray Cloth*. Taut later explained that his working relationship with Scheerbart navigated between the author's desire to free "buildings from the ordinary" and his own need to make structures "viable."[28]

Scheerbart's message was distilled and engaged by the German expressionists at the end of World War I. Four years after Scheerbart's death in 1915, the Crystal Chain, a circle of German expressionist architects led by Bruno Taut, cited Scheerbart as their spiritual leader, or "glaspapa."[29] This group used the visual arts to express political ideals in a world deadened by war. As there were few prospects for building after the war, they appropriated Scheerbart's architectural fantasies into experimental and exuberant ideas and images. Among the drawings to emerge from this movement are Taut's depictions of colored-glass landscapes in his visual poem *Alpine Architecture* (1919), Hans Scharoun's "Principles of Architecture" (1919), and Wassili Luckhardt's "Crystal on Sphere" (1920).[30]

The young Berlin architecture critic Adolf Behne also championed Scheerbart's ideas before and after World War I. Although Behne seems to have preferred Scheerbart's earlier fantastic works, he was nonetheless convinced of *The Gray Cloth*'s importance. In a piece written to celebrate Bruno Taut's achievement at the Cologne exhibition, Behne confidently exclaimed, "Everyone who knows German literature loves *The Gray Cloth*."[31] Despite its frequent attention from German literary scholars, Scheerbart's work was not included in the history of architectural modernism until the middle of the twentieth century, coincidentally the period in which *The Gray Cloth* is set.

In 1954, the architectural historian Sigfried Giedion mentioned Scheerbart in the context of Bruno Taut and the Werkbund Exhibition in his *Walter Gropius: Work and Teamwork*. Giedion described Taut's Glass House as the "embodiment of a poem by the fantastic poet, Paul Scheerbart."[32] Evidently not very familiar with Scheerbart, Giedion then transcribed a sentence from *Glass Architecture* that he had found quoted in Taut's *Die neue Baukunst* (The new building arts): "Glass architecture which turns the humble dwellings of men into cathedrals will exert the same beneficial influence over them."[33] In his 1959 essay "The Glass Paradise," Reyner Banham noted that Giedion made only cursory reference to Scheerbart in the Gropius book and excluded the poet completely from *Space, Time and Architecture*. Banham then reintroduced Scheerbart into architectural discourse as part of a challenge to make the history of architectural modernism "lifesize," writing:

> If one applies to [Scheerbart] the normal test for missing pioneers, that of prophecy uttered in the right ears at the right time, he scores more heavily than many other writers of his day. . . . In other words, he stood closer to the Seagram Building than Mies did in 1914.[34]

Banham was awed by the "unpredictable mixture of uninhibited vision and sharp practicality" found in Scheerbart's *Glass Architecture*, qualities he also found in Le Corbusier's *Towards a New Architecture*.[35] He perceived in Scheerbart's technological optimism an alignment with the modern movement. Banham pointed out, however, that the German author's anticlassical belief in the spiritual guidance of the "Orient" for the design of ornament and in the Gothic for integrated construction techniques placed him on a collision course with classically inspired modern thought. *The Gray Cloth* not only combines the practicality and vision correctly identified by Banham as relevant to the modern movement but also includes issues of broader relevance to culture and society.

Rosemarie Haag Bletter took up Banham's call to include Scheerbart in a growing canon of modern architecture. In her seminal essay of 1975, "Paul Scheerbart's Architectural Fantasies," Bletter examined Scheerbart's relationship to the development of German expressionist architecture through *The Gray Cloth* and *Glass Architecture*,[36] noting that Scheerbart "died the appointed court jester of his age to whom few had listened because his message was at once too cryptic and too intense."[37] The German journalist and scholar Mechthild Rausch has most closely followed in Bletter's footsteps. In addition to directing an early television show on glass architecture for German audiences, Rausch supplied an important critical commentary for and edited the 1986 reprint of *The Gray Cloth*; published collections of Scheerbart's letters, drawings, and short stories; and wrote an early biography of him. Scheerbart's popularity has also been enhanced through the publication of his complete works by Uli Kohnle and others at Edition Phantasia.[38]

The Gray Cloth: Vision and Ironic Humor

Published in 1914, under the shadows of World War I and Scheerbart's death, *The Gray Cloth* received relatively little attention from contemporary critics. In the only known literary review from the period, critic August Heinrich Kober adroitly captured the book's multiple nuances for readers of the influential Berlin journal *Das literarische Echo*:

Technical utopia (or perhaps more appropriately, technical futurism, since it only concerns itself with anticipated realities) and pure artistic formations of free adventures are balanced here in poetic harmony. . . . The whole book is a splendid color symphony. Technical realities and architectural dreams are exchanged in a dazzling magic of light, in wonderful glowing and harmonious colors. . . . One is reminded of Goethe's stories with their colors combined by an old poet and scientist, or of the romantics, whose color effects were as sacred as bright-hued chasubles.[39]

The critic discerned in Scheerbart's style an "epic simplicity" that weaves together the "enormity of the plot" and its "petty accidents." According to Kober, Scheerbart's greatest achievement was his ability to "touch modern man both emotionally and intellectually in equal measure." Kober remorsefully commented that *The Gray Cloth* demonstrates Scheerbart's unfulfilled literary potential and the power of his poetic imagination. He claimed that Scheerbart was first and foremost a poet, though often mistakenly considered a visionary along the lines of the "utopian Jules Verne." Kober suggested that in contrast to Scheerbart's earlier writings, which express "grotesquely eccentric distortion," *The Gray Cloth* reflects a refinement of Scheerbart's comic style into a "ripe old humor" found in the best German fairy tales.

In recognition of Scheerbart's pronounced irony, an excerpt of *The Gray Cloth* was selected to appear in a 1925 anthology of German literature entitled *Humor of Nations*.[40] Scheerbart was featured along with such eighteenth- and early-nineteenth-century satirists and ironists as Georg Christoph Lichtenberg, Jean Paul, and Heinrich von Kleist. This volume of German humor appeared with a companion volume on English humor, focusing on such authors as Jonathan Swift, Charles Dickens, and Oscar Wilde. Recent German reviewers have described Scheerbart's humor—at once classically German and intensely modern—as having the same freshness today as it did nearly ninety years ago.[41]

Scheerbart's ironic sensibility in *The Gray Cloth* is essential to the novel's implications and organizational structure. Because of its subtlety, Scheerbart's humorous irony is often difficult to grasp, the boundaries uncertain between vision and irony. While Scheerbart clearly endorses the globalization of glass architecture, his humorous position on its accompanying technologies and resultant fame and fashions confound straightforward interpretation. Like many other aspects of his writing, Scheerbart's irony relates to German romanticism—specifically to the work of Friedrich Schlegel (1772–1829), a principal theorist of ironic humor and the German novel.[42] *The Gray Cloth* reflects Schlegel's notion of irony as all-encompassing, a "mood that surveys everything and rises infinitely above all limitations, even above its own art and virtue."[43] Scheerbart's ironic language is rooted in the near future as an amplification of contemporary architectural and technological issues. He highlights his ironic effect through terse descriptions of characters and circumstances, engaging the reader in a dialogue between the fictional information presented by the author and the "real" emotions and expectations brought to the novel by the reader. Scheerbart choreographs these ruptures between fiction and reader as humorous moments throughout *The Gray Cloth*.

An instructive example of Scheerbart's irony can be found at the beginning of the novel when the first glimpse of sunshine radiates through the translucent walls of architect-protagonist Edgar Krug's Tower of Babel:

The splendor of the colored-glass ornament was so enhanced by the sun that one was at a loss for words to praise this wonder of color. Many visitors shouted repeatedly, "Delightful! Wonderful! Great! Incomparable!"

While the exclamations were repeated over and over, better-educated visitors found these and similar words quite distasteful. Fortunately, the exclamations stopped as soon as the sun crept back behind the clouds and there remained nothing left of it to see.[44]

In a manner typical of Scheerbart, this moment—which potentially contains much of the author's philosophy on the impact of glass architecture—is described with an unexpected twist: it was the "better-educated visitors" who were at a loss for words to express their delight, resentful of the heartfelt cries of the general public. Although a master of detail, Scheerbart enhances the spiritual aura of the scene by stressing that "nothing" is left to be seen following the interlude of sunshine. With their laconic style, Scheerbart's futuristic writings are very different from those of the French Jules Verne, the American Edward Bellamy, or the British H. G. Wells, who generally lacked his ironic humor in their extensively detailed and often technical descriptions. Instead, Scheerbart combines the social critique of Jonathan Swift and the fairy-tale structure of Clemens Brentano, two authors with whom he felt closely aligned.[45]

Another example of Scheerbart's ironic tone is found in an exchange between Edgar and Clara Krug and Clara's friend Amanda. Attempting to justify her husband's brusque behavior, Clara tells Amanda:

"My husband has such an inconsiderate, progressive nature that one must forgive his stubbornness. He is really consistent like a true hero in a novel. The name Edgar sounds too fitting for a novel."

"Oh!" shouted her husband, "precisely because it sounds so much like a novel do I go to a lot of trouble to veil what is like a novel in me."

"Oh, yes," then shouted Miss Amanda, "with your wife's gray cloth, isn't that true?"[46]

By playfully embedding the notion of a fictional hero within the fictional world itself, Scheerbart entices the reader to question the hermeneutic self-containment of the novel, in the process highlighting the complicit relationship between reader and author in the creation of fiction. At once intensely earnest and deeply suspicious of seriousness, Scheerbart both believed in and scoffed at Edgar's status as hero-architect and his consistency on the issue of gray and white. With fame and public recognition closely tied to Edgar's architecture and his personality, Scheerbart celebrates one of the central paradoxes of consumerist society, and lets the reader choose sides.

Architectural Globalism and Fame

The Gray Cloth offers insightful commentary on the implications of globalization and may be seen as a response to Wilhelmine Germany's embrace of expansion. Scheerbart relies heavily on emerging technologies and media—film, the international exposition, air travel—to address the dissemination of design values and the concomitant fame it provides. Such issues were integral to the formation of the Werkbund and to exchanges between modern European and American architects in the 1920s and thereafter. Scheerbart uses film in *The Gray Cloth* to demonstrate his interest in the potential of global representation and advertising. Introduced to the public at the 1900 Paris Universal Exposition, cinema soon proved to be a critical means for transmitting both political and architectural ideas.[47] Midway through the novel, Scheerbart introduces film in a humorous fashion in the form of a docudrama of the Krugs' marriage entitled "The Wedding of the Famous Architect," which uses actors and actresses to recreate the central event of the novel for global distribution.[48] This invention begs several questions. The film sensationalizes a wedding, purportedly in order to promote Edgar Krug's glass architecture among a European audience. Might Scheerbart similarly have intended to bring German readers into contact with glass architecture through the publication of *The Gray Cloth*, at a time when he was deeply involved with Bruno Taut and having difficulty finding a publisher for *Glass Architecture?* There is also an apparent disregard for precise detail in the making of the film. Clara complains that no care has been taken with the white and that her character in the film looks like a night owl. This has the comic effect of challenging the precise formulation of *The Gray Cloth* and of questioning the seriousness of the novel's title. The sensational film may be seen as an ironic commentary on the contemporary newsreel, which played formidable propagandistic and political roles during the Spanish-American and Boer wars and fomented surges of nationalism in Europe before World War I.[49] In *The Gray Cloth*, Scheerbart proposes a shift in cinematic subjects, away from expressions of nationalistic propaganda and toward promotional images of international design culture. This is achieved through the representation not only of architecture but also of a mobile upper-middle class that flies around the world constructing and inhabiting it. In reinforcing Edgar and Clara's fame, "The Wedding of the Famous Architect" highlights the commodification of this globalized medium, conflating messages of architecture and event.

The international dissemination of design is a central theme of the novel, and this is most evident in the many places Edgar Krug visits and colonizes with glass. No xenophobe, the Swiss Krug is first seen in Chicago, at an art exhibition restricted to American artists—perhaps an ironic reference to the contemporary arts and crafts exhibitions in Germany, which often showcased exclusively domestic production. Scheerbart's Chicago exhibition alludes also to the 1893 World's Columbian Exhibition that celebrated, among other things, the colonial efforts of Western Europe. For this exhibition, Germany constructed the most expensive and, by contemporary accounts, the most "remarkable" pavilion to showcase the country's design achievements.[50] Scheerbart's interest in internationalism is demonstrated in his fictive exhibition's central space, the "Tower of Babel." The name implies both the Middle Eastern roots Scheerbart ascribed to glass architecture and, with an ironic sensibility, the diversity of languages brought together within his vision of midcentury modernism.[51] By opening the novel in Chicago, legendary as a world's fair city, and ending it at Lüneburg Heath, site of a fictional world's fair, Scheerbart evoked much of the fantasy, futurism, and commercialism of international expositions.

In *The Gray Cloth*, Scheerbart locates architectural construction within a global, geopolitical framework. Edgar Krug's path through the novel has significant imperialistic overtones as it moves across remnants of the British Empire. While the United States, Australia, and India—sites visited by Krug—were or had been three of Britain's largest colonies, Fiji, Borneo, Ceylon (modern Sri Lanka), and Malta were all either fully or partially under British control at one time or another. Antarctica was discovered and investigated by the British explorer Edward Bransfield in 1820, and the Kuria Muria Islands, located off the coast of Oman in the Arabian Sea, were ceded to Britain in 1854. Scheerbart interprets places he had never seen, a practice recurrent in earlier German Orientalist literature. As Edward Said points out, both Goethe and Schlegel, two of Scheerbart's heroes from the romantic period, wrote about the Orient without ever leaving Europe, and in this respect were typical of German scholars who generally relied on "texts, myths, ideas and languages gathered from the Orient by imperial Britain and France."[52]

Scheerbart formulates and tests his concept of fashion and colored-glass architecture against an intellectualized notion of Asia through the characters of the Japanese Marquise Fi-Boh and the Chinese patron Li-Tung. Fi-Boh becomes Clara's friend and a fan of her tower-organ playing. She consoles Clara and visits her in India, accompanied by a retinue of guests. Li-Tung, on the other hand, is Edgar's primary patron. After offering Edgar a large commission, Li-Tung, it is revealed, steals the Maltese collection of "Oriental

weapons," which results in a global scandal and, ultimately, the transformation of the weapons museum into a museum of colored-glass
architecture that features Edgar's work. Li-Tung defiantly defends his
crime as a means of supporting the architect's reputation, stating with
powerful irony that "fame needs to be revitalized. . . . That's why I
took care of it. Revitalization is important. Otherwise, fame goes
sour."[53] Although both Fi-Boh and Li-Tung express their great appre-
ciation of Krug's glass architecture, neither tolerates the architect's insistence that Clara wear gray garments: Fi-Boh calls her uniform an
"old ghostly shroud,"[54] while Li-Tung insists on purchasing clothing for
Clara during her visit to his home. Many Orientalist writers have similarly endowed their characters with autonomous opinions.[55] Through
the voices of Li-Tung and Fi-Boh, Scheerbart questions the unilateral
aesthetic authority of the West on the subject of glass architecture.

The airship, one of the most conspicuous elements of the Krugs'
lifestyle, is also critical to Scheerbart's conception of international design and amply illustrates the importance of technology to his vision.
Airships not only provide habitation, transportation, and a perspective
on the world, but also a connection to the global community of air
travelers, who communicate through light signals, telegraph, and re-
mote control.

An invention less than two decades old in 1914, the airship had
already sparked the imagination and pride of the German middle
class.[56] When a zeppelin was sighted over southern Germany in 1908,
the *Schwäbischer Merkur* reported: "One feels its power: we are overcome by a nervous trembling as we follow the flight of the ship in the
air. As only with the great artistic experiences, we feel ourselves up-
lifted. Some people rejoice, others weep."[57] The conflation of the airship with artistic experience is seen in *The Gray Cloth* when crowds
listen to Clara's internationally acclaimed tower-organ concerts from
airships hovering above.

Unlike his characters, in particular Edgar Krug, who supposedly "knew the development of the airship perfectly"[58] and revered its contribution, Scheerbart expressed fear that the militarism implicit in the development of air technology would cause international calamity. In contrast to his descriptions of the peaceful civilian use of the airship in *The Gray Cloth*, Scheerbart reacted strongly against Germany's use of these vehicles to carry bombs. He was convinced that air attacks, unlike conventional means of warfare, which required the conquest of territory, could destroy civic and cultural centers well within the borders of countries in conflict. Scheerbart predicted, with perspicacity, that the devastation caused by air-based weaponry would be the greatest the world had ever seen.

Gender, Fashion, and Architecture

The Gray Cloth had several working titles, each reflecting Scheerbart's changing priorities. In December 1912 he dubbed it a "novel with one thousand glass palaces," highlighting the story's vision of colored-glass buildings.[59] By spring of the following year, when he was looking for individuals to form his Society of Glass Architecture, he alluded to it as an "architects novel." Just before its publication in 1914, however, in a letter to Bruno Taut, Scheerbart referred to the tale as "Müller's 'Ladies Novel,'" perhaps with a note of dismay at his publisher's request for a fictional piece in lieu of *Glass Architecture*.[60]

The ultimate title's sartorial formula is somewhat opaque as an indicator of the novel's concerns. It is the work's first and greatest irony, implying a critique of standardization, simplicity, uniformity, practicality, and, perhaps above all, modernity. It brings to mind the static uniforms of nurses and nuns, and, of course, of middle-class European men—all antitheses of diverse and ever-changing mainstream women's fashions.[61] With its reference to one of the novel's oblique concepts, the title's form contrasts greatly with Scheerbart's tendency throughout his career to name works after their protagonists (e.g., *Rakkóx the Billionaire*, *Münchhausen and Clarissa*, *Lesabéndio*) or after a straightforward narrative theme (*e.g.*, *Paradise: Homeland of Art*, *The Great Revolution*, *The Perpetual Motion Machine*).

In subtitling *The Gray Cloth* "A Ladies Novel," Scheerbart imbued the work with complex gender significance, some of which may be understood by reference to his 1912 "The Light Club of Batavia: A Ladies Short Story."[62] Published as Scheerbart started work on *The Gray Cloth*, this tale is set in 1909 at the Hôtel de l'Europe in Batavia (The Netherlands). The story has five characters: Mrs. Hortense Pline, an engineer; her companion, Mrs. Arabelle Thackeray; Mr. Hartung, an architect who builds only glass structures; and two wealthy Americans, Mr. Benjamin and Mr. Krumhübel, the clients for a "light" spa to be constructed of glass. The humorous plot unfolds as Mrs. Pline expresses her desire for more light during the night, the absence of which she inexplicably deems "the most striking sign of our times" and "the most modern disease."[63] Mr. Hartung responds to the engineer's request by proposing that the spa be built in an abandoned mine. Mrs. Pline knows of one such mine nearby and quickly forms the "Light Club of Batavia," an organization to help realize the "fantastic plans in [her] head." Although fearing that the club will not be viable, the architect nonetheless offers his assistance. To this Mrs. Pline responds:

Please Mr. Hartung, . . . do not fear too soon. One invariably becomes fearful soon enough. Men are always afraid. That is no sign of courage. We women are less fearful. Therefore, we too, on our own, bring a bit of progress to world history. What would the entire world be if it were not for women's courage?[64]

After this scolding, Mrs. Pline explains the project to the others over dinner, describing the interior of the light spa she envisions and ultimately constructs. It features backlit glass walls, floors, ceilings, and columns, which form spaces serviced by colorful elevators with Tiffany-glass walls.

The subtitle "A Ladies Short Story" reflects the critical role of women in "The Light Club of Batavia," a tale that demonstrates Scheerbart's belief—at least in his fictional world—that women are as capable as men of creating extraordinary colored-glass constructions.[65] In *The Gray Cloth*, Clara Krug is recognized as an artist in her own right, despite her concomitant role as a fashion accessory. The narrative reminds one of Scheerbart's earlier works, including *Paradise: Homeland of Art*, which involves a search for spiritual healing through the creation of colored-glass environments. Although some have concluded that *The Gray Cloth*'s subtitle suggests a less thoughtful form of literature, the comparable subtitle of the "Light Club" and the seriousness of that work support a more subtle reading of gender and sensationalism.[66]

The novel's subtitle may also be seen as an homage to the author's wife Anna, to whom he dedicated *The Gray Cloth*. Anna Scheerbart often socialized with her husband's literary acquaintances, and the couple appeared together on photographic postcards of Berlin's famous literary *Stammtischen*.[67] She was also the author of at least two newspaper articles published in *Die Frau und ihre Zeit* (Woman and her time) in 1909 and one in the *Berliner Tageblatt* in 1927.[68] Through *The Gray Cloth*'s subtitle and dedication, perhaps Scheerbart wished to highlight parallels between his literature-based life and marriage and the architecture-based lives of Edgar and Clara.

At the outset of the novel, the critical issues of fashion, gender, and architecture suggested in the title and subtitle are laid out with structural simplicity. Unlike Scheerbart's earlier novels, in which events often unfold in a languorous and spiritual flow, *The Gray Cloth* adopts a fast, staccato pace through time and space. Ferocious organ music sets the tempo for the prose and introduces Clara, the organist, to Edgar Krug. No measurements are taken of Clara's gray and white clothing, and the technical formula dissolves at once into an abstract aesthetic discourse on fashion. The ten percent formula is a metonym for the construction of Clara's clothing and alludes to the mathematical efficiency associated with functional architecture. Krug's own notion of beauty in fashion is bound to what he considers suitable for glass architecture. In an ingenious way, Scheerbart thus places his finger on one of most forceful elements of modernity, the very subjectivity of the functionality and materiality that bound it into a conceptual whole. With the formula, he foregrounds such subjectivity against mass media, globalization, and new transportation technologies.

In *The Gray Cloth*, Scheerbart weighs into the long-standing critical discussion of architecture and fashion initiated by Gottfried Semper, who remarked that "the beginning of building coincides with the beginning of textiles."[69] By 1914 this dialogue had intensified as several German-speaking architects, including Henry van de Velde, Josef Hoffmann, and Peter Behrens, were designing women's clothing as part of complete design environments. Together, garments, interior furnishings, and architecture created a *Gesamtkunstwerk* or total work of art. These designers considered women's clothing so important to architecture that the famed German Werkbund promoter Karl Ernst Osthaus stated: "Woe to such a lady who would enter such a room in a dress that was not artistically suitable."[70] The relationship between architecture and fashion was also apparent to the critics of *Gesamtkunstwerk*. Adolf Loos asked: "But have you never noticed the strange correspondence between the exterior dress of people and the exterior of buildings? Is the tasselled robe not appropriate to the Gothic Style and the wig to the Baroque?"[71] Scheerbart did not closely adhere to either Osthaus's or Loos's position. Rather, he maintained the critical and indefinable notion of suitability common to both.

He was, moreover, able to relish the rich irony of these antagonistic positions by proposing in *The Gray Cloth* that contemporary women's outfits be fixed and unchanging—and thereby modern—while architecture was colorful, vibrant, and expressive—and thereby fashionable. The dichotomy between fashion and architecture in *The Gray Cloth* may be seen, though, as opposed to the ideology of *Gesamtkunstwerk*. The British arts and crafts magazine *The Craftsman* noted: "If we are going to simplify life, simplicity is not for one phase and extravagance for another. It is of no use to build houses of the kind that reduce labor, and make dresses of the kind that use up all the hours we have saved in our wise architecture."[72] On the contrary, Clara Krug remarks in the novel: "It is better to have a colorful house than colorful clothing. The former makes all of life colorful, while the latter only serves vanity and makes away with money that should be for building houses. Edgar was right about the gray cloth."[73]

Clara's position as the wearer and bearer of the gray cloth is also tied to the profession of architecture and, specifically, to the architect-client relationship. Clara considers her "first success" to be the fact that her gray clothing placates a Cypriot client, who is wary of Edgar's single-minded enthusiasm for color.[74] The idea that clients had to be lured into using colored-glass architecture was reiterated by Adolf Behne, who commented favorably on Bruno Taut's ability to carry out the promotion and education necessary to achieve the modern ideal.[75] On this point Behne quoted Clara's lines from *The Gray Cloth*: "You must seduce people into using colors. I understand that this is no small task. And—the gray cloth that I wear should help persuade the client toward this."[76]

Clara's clothing also masks her femininity, effectively reducing distinctions of gender between her and Edgar. Scheerbart has the Krugs actually put into practice the position expressed by Adolf Loos at the end of his 1898 essay "Ladies' Fashion":

But we are approaching a new and greater time. No longer by an appeal to sensuality, but rather by economic independence earned through work will the woman bring about her equal status with the man. The woman's value or lack of value will no longer fall or rise according to the fluctuation of sensuality. Then velvet and silk, flowers and ribbons, feathers and paints will fail to have their effect. They will disappear.[77]

Noting the distinction between Loos's interiors and exteriors, architectural historian Mary McLeod has observed that this architect's position was restrictive and paradoxical. It effectively separated the modern public sphere, stripped of ornament and sensuality, from the private world of play and eroticism.[78] Scheerbart distinguished himself from Loos by blurring the relationship between interior and exterior through the use of colored-glass translucency. He also proposed celebrating fame, appearance, and pretense as a means of promoting colored-glass architecture, noted for its truth, content, and integrity. Grasping the subtleties of the media-infused world to a degree Loos rarely did, Scheerbart's characters in *The Gray Cloth* use manipulative means, including advertisement and subterfuge, to perpetuate modern architecture.

Paul Scheerbart's Other Architecture Fictions

Among Scheerbart's fictional work, *The Gray Cloth* is one of his most complex explorations of architecture. But his interest in materials and space extends back to his first novel, *Paradise: Homeland of Art*, published in 1889 and then republished by the author himself in 1893.[79] Permeated by faith in the power of art to convey cultural ideals, this sweet and fantastic story is constructed around a group of "devils" who leave their home in Hell on a guided tour of paradise accompanied by witches and angels. A thinly veiled allusion to life on earth, the parable unfolds in two parallel narrations, one in prose and the other in verse, both from the perspective of an unnamed poet-devil. These tales reveal the beginnings of the richly descriptive style Scheerbart would develop during the course of his career. Experiences of color, material, light, and glass are first described in prose "reality" and then reflected in verse descriptions by the poet-devil narrator. In *Paradise*, Scheerbart presents art as "a mirror of the world," a distorted and manipulated likeness whose meaning can be understood only within the specific context of its production.[80] The author's belief in the nexus of nature and architecture is apparent in this passage from *Paradise*, characteristic of Scheerbart's writing in its descriptive brevity:

In the red luster of the setting sun, we approached the diamond, the most beautiful mountain on the highest of all ridges,

> The diamond
>
> The twinkling mountain
>
> Star dew!
>
> Ray buildings!
>
> Pearl suppleness!
>
> Shining lightning!
>
> Edge cone,
>
> Cube throne,
>
> Wonder lives
>
> In the reflective stones;
>
> More brightly shines
>
> The glimmering light,
>
> The shimmering poetry
>
> Glowing in the slippery smooth
>
> Glass roof.[81]

Scheerbart expresses here a notion of artistic and spiritual radiance that infuses materiality, landscape, building, and poetry, all within glass construction. This would have particular influence over the later expressionists. In fact, in 1918, some thirty years after the publication of *Paradise*, Bruno Taut reflected sentiments similar to Scheerbart's ethereal unification of the arts within architecture in his "Architecture Program" for the Arbeitsrat für Kunst (Work Council for Art, part of the short-lived Republic of Workers' Councils in revolutionary Munich):

Art!—that is a great thing, when it exists. Today this art does not exist. The fragmented tendencies can only find their way back to a single unity under the wings of a new architecture, with each individual discipline playing its part in the building process. Then there will be no division between the applied arts and sculpture or painting; everything will be one: architecture.[82]

Scheerbart's conception of the relationship between man, nature, and architecture loosely follows the spiritual teachings of the influential German physicist and philosopher Gustav Theodor Fechner (1801–1887). As the founder of psychophysics, a movement devoted to the search for a scientific relationship between sensation and stimulus, Fechner believed not only in an ultimate harmony between body and mind, spirit and consciousness, but also in the prominence of architecture among the arts. "Fechner," noted the Dutch architect H. P. Berlage, "always ranks architecture along with applied arts as being among those arts that also serve a purpose; they are the arts of repose."[83] Scheerbart's insistence on individual artistic transcendence mirrors Fechner's teaching that after death a "new universal luminousness" guides the soul to perceive "the true relations between unity and diversity, connection and separation, harmony and discord."[84] Most notably, Scheerbart attributed his belief that "stars really are living things" to Fechner, and he developed several astral-themed works based on this idea.[85]

Scheerbart's most complete expression of this conviction is found in *Liwûna and Kaidôh: A Souls' Novel* (1902).[86] This deeply spiritual piece traces the adventures of Kaidôh, a heavenly soul who floats through the universe by wiggling his toes in search of truths he believes are "greater and larger" than those he already knows. Very early in his adventures, Kaidôh encounters Liwûna, a large, metamorphosing being who shows him worlds of scale beyond what he has ever imagined. Liwûna, we later learn, is the embodiment of Kaidôh's desire. She gradually discloses the infinite scale of the universe, disappearing only when Kaidôh is transformed both physically and spiritually through his discovery of a higher manifestation of truth beyond desire. Over the course of this revelation, massive colored columns beneath cupolas of glass and other architectural constructions appear in space, at times nearly indistinguishable from the asteroids and stars into which they are set.[87]

In July 1912, Scheerbart completed the manuscript of *Lesabéndio: An Asteroid Novel*, which was published with illustrations by the well-known expressionist artist Alfred Kubin.[88] Scheerbart's last astral novel, *Lesabéndio* was highly treasured by Walter Benjamin for presenting "the best of all worlds."[89] It recounts life on Pallas, a double-cone-shaped asteroid, whose peaceful inhabitants, without government or institutions, unite to discover what lies beyond a luminous cloud above one end of their world. Lesabéndio, a Pallasian astronomer, convinces the asteroid's residents to construct a huge observation tower toward this end. The seven-mile-high tower is eventually completed, and Lesabéndio, upon climbing the tower, is dramatically transformed into a celestial being, an asteroid in his own right. In the spirit of Eden, the process of transformation introduces the pain of knowledge to Lesabéndio and the other Pallasians, thereby altering the paradisal nature of life in their world. Pallas represents a purity of life beyond that achievable through earthly political or economic systems. The struggle to attain higher knowledge of worlds beyond those already known is represented by the desire to construct observation towers and undertake adventures. Overtones of cultural and intellectual imperialism course through the novel, the most obvious being the appropriation of ten miniscule inhabitants of a nearby star to assist Lesabéndio with his task. One Pallasian explorer visits Earth and returns to his planet, horrified that people not only killed and ate other "less intelligent creatures" but also killed each other in massive quantities with guns and swords.[90] This position reflects Scheerbart's pacifist tendencies, as expressed, for example, in his *The Development of Air Militarism and the Dissolution of European Land Armies, Fortifications, and Navies* (1910), in which he writes: "The mere contemplation of such arts of war can cause a nervous breakdown."[91]

During his lifetime, Scheerbart was probably best known for the short articles he contributed to Berlin's rapidly growing daily newspaper trade,[92] including the popular *Berliner Tageblatt* and the *Hamburger Fremdenblatt*.[93] In these journalistic pieces, Scheerbart developed his ideas on glass architecture and formulated many of the narrative structures later used in *The Gray Cloth*.[94] His work appeared frequently in the feuilleton section of the papers, a literary forum focusing on fiction, reviews, or general entertainment that flowered in the German press from the 1890s until the 1930s.[95] This type of regular column catered to the Wilhelmine sense of the absurd, teetering between the cultural and the quirky news story or, as was repeatedly the case with Scheerbart's contributions, the fictional morality tale. Scheerbart's writing style was clearly appropriate for the feuilleton, which historian Peter Fritzsche describes as having served up "an excess of details" in "shorter and shorter fragments that pile up at a faster and faster pace . . . in an almost telegraphic style."[96] Scheerbart's early journalistic pieces, written between 1889 and 1893, focus on topics commonly found in the feuilleton sections, including art, architecture, and culture in Berlin. His articles from this period consider such themes as the Panorama in Berlin's Hohenzollern-Galerie, the exhibitions at Berlin's Egyptian Museum, and the use of polychromy in architectural facades.[97] The latter topic was addressed in an illustrated essay of 1893, "Berlin's Architectonic Sculpture," in which Scheerbart remarked favorably on contemporary buildings that made the city "ever more colorful."[98] Although his cultural criticism prefigures his descriptive, nonfiction prose in *Glass Architecture*, his short, fictional essays in the feuilleton sections foreshadow the international adventures of *The Gray Cloth*.

One of the best examples of the latter is a short story entitled "The Congress of Architects: A Parliament Story," first published in 1913 in the *Berliner Tageblatt*, then reprinted after Scheerbart's death in Bruno Taut's journal *Frühlicht* (Dawn).[99] Presumably written following Scheerbart's completion of *Lesabéndio* and while he was working on *The Gray Cloth*, the piece describes a global convention dedicated to the advocacy of an international architectural building style. It contains noteworthy connections to *The Gray Cloth*, including a somewhat realistic futurist setting, an international array of characters, and a framing of architectural discourse within the context of fame. Perhaps most important, the short story anticipates Scheerbart's skillful use of narrative in *The Gray Cloth* as a means of exploring the complex relationships between architectural construction and cultural change.

Set in the second quarter of the twentieth century near the German town of Brandenburg, the story recounts a fictional meeting of international architects and administrators to discuss the construction of glass architecture in their respective regions. The congress begins on a spiritual note, with a call by the "great architect and secret governmental advisor Krummbach" for "brightly colored, translucent, double-glass walls . . . that do not close us off from the great, infinite

universe. For the greatest is the boundless." The unbridled spiritual-
ism of the European delegates is countered by America's millionaire
representative, the chairman of the congress, who exclaims that phi-
losophizing on colored glass holds "no meaning for the practical
American."[100] Representatives from Italy, France, Spain, China, and
Turkey then report that construction of steel and glass is a high prior-
ity among their constituents. France, however, relays that its military's
intention to bomb brick buildings in order to replace them with glass
and steel has met with citizen protest. Japan extols the resistance of
glass and steel to both earthquakes and bombs, while Peru discusses
the adaptability of glass architecture to the tropics with the addition
of cloth shading devices. In a humorous twist, a German bureaucrat
expresses concern about the comfort of glass architecture and furniture that rely on structural steel. He is informed that the surfaces of
the steel are to be covered in enamel. Like Dutch ovens that are similarly constructed, it is argued, the new steel designs will soon feel
comfortable.

Scheerbart frames the story within a discussion between a father
and his son, revolving around whether the son should become an engineer, as he wishes, or an architect. After watching the congress from
afar, the son decides to be both engineer and architect. To this his
father replies, "You can only become famous as an architect. . . .
Promise me that you will take great pains to do so!"[101] The conviction
that twentieth-century glass architecture will match the international
success of nineteenth-century engineering forms a central motif in
The Gray Cloth. It presages, by more than a decade, Le Corbusier's
closely aligned observation in *Towards a New Architecture* that the engineer "achieves harmony," whereas the architect "realizes an order
which is a pure creation of his spirit" and allows us to "experience the
sense of beauty."[102] Along these lines, Scheerbart's fictional Edgar

Krug shares a number of Le Corbusier's traits, including an interest in technology—particularly flight—a globalized architectural practice, a fanatical ideology, and a remarkable unity of vision.

Although, in 1910, Scheerbart had published a rather technical treatise, replete with diagrams and images, on his ongoing project to discover a perpetual motion machine, his partial transformation from a poet of fantasy to a technical writer surprised many. In fact, the editors of the *Berliner Tageblatt* prefaced Scheerbart's description of Taut's glass pavilion with the somewhat apologetic words:

Paul Scheerbart, the poet of cosmic fantasies and grotesque dreams, appears in the following statement on an unusual side. The interesting idea for a glass house that he himself had dreamt of in many of his works should appear at the Cologne Werkbund Exhibition next year. To the realization of his dream, the greatest event of his life, as he calls it, he dedicates this "Preliminary Report," about whose technical details we do not want to argue with the poet.[103]

The subsequent article presents an uncharacteristically sober account of Bruno Taut's previous experience with exhibition buildings and includes detailed descriptions of the form and materials of the new structure. Later in 1914, Scheerbart reused much of the material for an essay on Taut's pavilion in the professional German engineering periodical *Technische Monatshefte*.[104]

Conclusion   In his essay "The Storyteller," Walter Benjamin wrote: "The 'meaning of life' is really the center about which the novel moves. But the quest for it is no more than the initial expression of perplexity with which its reader sees himself living this written life."[105] Applying Benjamin's dictum to the fictitious *The Gray Cloth*, readers may find themselves deeply perplexed. What is to be taken seriously, what is not? Why is character development minimal and fragmented? Although the politics, social observations, and even geography of *The Gray Cloth* may be considered outlandish, the novel carries important implications for our understanding of the multifarious positions and directions of the early twentieth century and modern architecture. To understand this work, one must employ a multidisciplinary approach to the analysis of architecture and culture. As this introduction has demonstrated, such dialogues may focus on the relationship between architecture and internationalism, the cult of the hero-architect, fashion, building materials, and construction techniques, to note just a few possibilities. Scheerbart used his powerful sense of humor to ask provocative questions about the world that produced the nonfictional Edgar Krugs of the twentieth century, such as Rem Koolhaas, Zaha Hadid, Norman Foster, Richard Meier, and Frank Gehry. How are the narratives of their lives constructed within the context of twentieth-century architecture, politics, and media? Our most renowned contemporary architects are featured in glossy monographs and lifestyle magazines and an array of consumer ads. Their presence secures public attention and raises awareness of the architectural profession. Yet embedded within their fame are difficult modern paradoxes of style and content, globalism and regionalism, and socioeconomic inequality. That *The Gray Cloth*, a fairy tale of a honeymoon written at the outset of the twentieth century, can still arouse so many questions demonstrates the endurance of what Walter Gropius considered the "wisdom and beauty" of Paul Scheerbart's work.

NOTES ON THE TRANSLATION AND DRAWINGS

In many ways, my method for translating this novel paralleled an architectural design process based on respecting and ultimately occupying an existing condition. As I crafted a new book from the original German text, I attempted to maintain as much of the author's meaning, writing style, and spirit as possible. At times this involved a process of negotiation between the original German and the new English text that resulted in creative compromises as well as unforeseen discoveries. I found, therefore, that translating was analogous to creating a new structure through which the reader may inhabit the original work of art.

Paul Scheerbart was as innovative with language as he was with ideas. A master of wordplay, he frequently used foreign or invented phrases to express new conditions. Terms relating to technological inventions, such as "air chauffeur," "snow scrapers," "automobile sled," and "air conditioner," were anything but common parlance in 1914. Invoking internationalism, Scheerbart often combined German, French, and English phrases. He frequently switched between German and English titles, referring at will to Edgar Krug, for example, as both "Herr Krug" and "Mr. Krug." I have attempted in this translation to maintain as much of the author's idiosyncratic word choice and language structure as possible, including Scheerbart's use of "and" as well as the em-dash to introduce phrases. I have also maintained the sectional divisions of the original novel, marked by three asterisks spread across the page.

The accompanying pastel drawings are meant to challenge the reader to consider complex spatial configurations inspired by Scheerbart's narrative. These visual vignettes are not intended as illustrations; rather, they should be seen as explorations of issues found in the novel, including color, light, landscape, structure, and materiality. As responses to verbal cues in the text, the images foreground complex relationships between reading and drawing, imagining and creating, landscape and architecture. For example, just as Scheerbart's structures often appear to grow from the ground, so the landscapes in the drawings become architectural, and the distinctions between the two are at times difficult to discern.

The drawings were created using a process of masking and rendering each element of the image. The sharpness of the edges and the intensity of the color within are suggestive of the leading and stained glass of a Gothic window. After the process of rendering and covering, the drawings were "excavated" and brought to light for the first time as a total composition. The drawings, then, can be seen as an attempt to follow Scheerbart in visualizing the figure through an unpredictable process of creation.

THE GRAY CLOTH AND TEN PERCENT WHITE: A LADIES NOVEL

BY PAUL SCHEERBART

To my dear bear, Frau Anna Scheerbart

Near Chicago on Lake Michigan, American sculptors and decorative artists had arranged an exhibition. There were only works of silver on display. It was the middle of the twentieth century. The architect Edgar Krug had built the exhibition hall out of glass and iron. It was opening day and, with lively gestures, the architect led his friend, the lawyer Walter Löwe, around the enormous halls, pointing out details of the architecture and ornament.

The colossal walls were made completely out of colored glass, with colored ornament, so that only subdued daylight shone into the interior. It was raining outside. The sun was not shining. But the colors of the glass gleamed powerfully nonetheless.

Herr Edgar Krug said quietly:

"Indeed, the silver sculpture contrasts wonderfully with the colorful glass walls. One could not find better surroundings for this quantity of silver pieces. True, don't you think?"

"I only fear," responded Herr Löwe, "that the surroundings will seem to be too big. One has the impression that there are not many works of silver here. They disappear almost completely in the huge hall. You talk about the vast quantity—that seems a little strange to me."

"Excuse me," answered the architect, "there are almost one hundred thousand pieces here."

"Too few!" shouted the lawyer. "Your colorfully ornamented glass walls attract most of the attention. Look around you, the whole world marvels at your glass walls. But no one pays any attention to the silver works. You have conquered the silver sculptures. I congratulate you."

"Quiet! Quiet!" whispered the architect, "one of the artists could be nearby."

Tower of Babel, Chicago, United States

They found themselves on a large and fairly wide "embankment" that rose high in the middle of the large hall. On this so-called embankment were the largest pieces of silver—the sculptural works. The walls were very far from the embankment. Here the hall had the effect of being very large—and the silver works appeared to be very small, horribly small. Actually, it was generally observed that the colored-glass surroundings turned out to be a little too big—but no one felt that was something to complain about. The artists themselves were completely delighted with the colorful surroundings, and they said as much to the architect. Each compliment pleased him very much.

Around midday, when the sun became visible outside, there was some commotion in the exhibition hall. The splendor of the colored-glass ornament was so enhanced by the sun that one was at a loss for words to praise this wonder of color. Many visitors shouted repeatedly, "Delightful! Wonderful! Great! Incomparable!"

While the exclamations were repeated over and over, better-educated visitors found these and similar words quite distasteful. Fortunately, the exclamations stopped as soon as the sun crept back behind the clouds and there remained nothing left of it to see.

At one end of the long "embankment," which was really a four-story building in the middle of the glass hall, there hung a long, gray, single-colored pleated curtain. At present, it was pulled aside revealing a huge organ, also in gray but with some gold in the many rails of its balcony. With finely curved bends, these rails enclosed the organ like a net so that it wasn't shown to its best advantage.

Very delicate organ music began.

Many visitors sat on the embankment in the niches and listened. As the organ suddenly began to roar loudly, others took the elevators to the lower floors where the sound was less intense.

There was an intermission after the first piece, and Herr Walter Löwe introduced a lady to the architect: Miss Amanda Schmidt from Chicago.

The lady did not make a favorable impression on the architect. She wore a dark violet velvet dress with carmine red and chrysolite green cuffs and trim.

Herr Edgar Krug said softly to the lawyer:

"I'm really supposed to be the only one here discussing colors. The ladies should be more discreet in their outfits—out of respect for my glass windows."

"Your fame," responded the lawyer, "has made you a little pretentious. You should curb your lust for power a bit."

At that moment, three drumbeats resounded through the space. Then a pair of choir songs emanated from the balcony of the organ; the organ itself projected out over the human voices. Then three drumbeats resounded again. And simultaneously the electric lights in all of the walls were illuminated.

It made an enormous effect.

Along with this, the organ roared with such a stormy rhythm that all the seated visitors involuntarily sprang up and stared at the dazzling color magic, absorbing the powerful tones of the organ with open mouths. Herr Walter Löwe pointed out to Miss Schmidt that almost all of the visitors had their mouths thrown open. And the woman laughed out loud. Herr Krug remained completely serious.

*   *   *

When the organ was again quiet, everyone flooded together, laughing and gesticulating. And the three traveled to the lower floors where the smaller works in silver were displayed.

There were cabinets here from which one could not see the colored windows of the hall. A subdued monochromatic light glowed from the walls, from columns and large lamps. The single color was calming.

The favored sculpture of the mid-twentieth century depicted an aquatic motif. The Japanese veil fish[1] had provided the inspiration. A type of goldfish, these veil fish suspend their fins from their bellies like flowing garments.

Their heads, however, were not those of fish. Instead, other heads had been given them—those of lions, bulls, and, above all, humans. The heads were often so abstract that one could no longer discern the original inspiration. But the small fin-monsters nonetheless appeared to be very graceful.

Herr Krug remained standing before one of these compositions for a particularly long time, stating finally:

"In this example one does not know if it is supposed to be a lion's head or a transformed human head. In any case, the beard and the eyebrows are also flowing fins. And the side fin encases the entire body—like a cloak. There are, moreover, many cloaks over one another. Yes, I would like to buy it."

"Are you," asked Miss Amanda Schmidt, "already prepared to buy it? That would indeed please the artists very much. I thought you would think about it longer and first look at a few more. There are many better compositions."

Herr Krug then said somewhat sharply:

"My dearest lady, I am very independent. And therefore, I would like the purchase to be arranged immediately."

He called an attendant.

Herr Walter Löwe smiled.

---

1. The veil fish may be a reference to the tropical veil carp or *Pterolebias longipinnis*.

Miss Amanda Schmidt looked very serious. Five minutes later, a small medallion was set on the fine silver piece, glittering with the notice "sold."

The trifle cost five hundred dollars.

The piece had to remain in its place until the end of the exhibition. This Herr Krug sincerely regretted.

Miss Amanda extended her hand to the architect and said:

"My greatest thanks!"

"What for?" asked Herr Krug.

"To be sure," responded the lady, "you have been so distracted today by your own great success that you have not yet inquired about me."

Herr Walter smiled again.

"Why," shouted Herr Krug, "how could I have simply ventured to inquire? Indeed, that would have been offensive."

"But," answered Miss Amanda, "you would have heard that I have exhibited. I am, in fact, a sculptor—I work almost exclusively in silver."

Herr Krug was quite embarrassed.

"Oh," he said with regret, "I'm very sorry that I did not consider your work earlier."

The lawyer turned around, held his handkerchief to his mouth, then laughing, he shouted:

"Edgar, you have already bought the most beautiful of Miss Amanda's work."

Edgar stammered something but did not yet understand. Then Miss Amanda spoke, pointing to the purchased work.

"I made it."

For the next five minutes there was great laughter, many handshakes, apologies and compliments, etc. . . .

Finally, Miss Amanda spoke with complete seriousness.

"You have not yet been very kind to me personally—only to my work. This last kindness has compensated for everything. But for your behavior you must do a little something for me. Join us for dinner—up at the top of the Tower of Babel. You have already endured my friend's company—she is Clara Weber, the organ player. Listen, she is playing again."

All three listened.

And Herr Krug was in complete agreement with everything. They looked at the time, and Miss Amanda indicated that Fräulein Clara Weber would be free in an hour.

The men were a bit thirsty.

They drank some seltzer with whiskey, which was close at hand.

Then Herr Löwe suggested that they explore the roofs of the exhibition building on the exhibition train.

And that they did.

One had to use a pair of elevators, first to go down and then to go up again. And thus one emerged upon a great roof plateau from which small cars traveled out and around the great cupola of the central palace. The architect drove with Miss Amanda and Herr Löwe in one of these cars. There were double walls everywhere, and the exhibit appeared to be colorfully ornamented. And from the outside, the exhibition halls were even more impressive than from the inside.

One saw the very colorful reflection of the palaces in Lake Michigan. Like hummingbirds, dragonflies, and butterflies the countless colors flickered along the moving waves of the lake. And the full moon glowed. It too was reflected in the water. Several airplanes traveled over the lake, letting their colorful floodlights frolic.

"A very colorful picture!" said Herr Krug. And he lit himself a cigarette.

*   *   *

The Tower of Babel stood in the middle of the Round Palace, on the edge of whose roof the three had been driving.

The Tower of Babel had thirty platforms, with a circular platform at the top. On all of the floors were refreshment rooms. It was most impressive up on the circular platform. One saw the colorful, electrically lit glass walls on all sides. And down from the ceiling hung many thousand-colored lights that lowered slowly and then rose back up. Also, the glass wall darkened piece by piece, and the light was constantly changing. This metamorphosis of colored light occurred so slowly and subtly that it was in no way disturbing.

Herr Krug was extremely surprised by the appearance of Fräulein Clara Weber. The lady wore a simple gray garment with ten-percent-white trim.

Herr Krug was immediately enchanted by this outfit and said so, again apologizing to Miss Amanda for not finding her colorful clothing beautiful—since it did not work well with his glass walls—for in Herr Krug's view only a gray outfit with ten percent white suited his glass walls.

They spoke about this quite a bit, and the four became ever more animated.

*　　　　*　　　　*

After tortoise soup, oysters, and caviar, the four ate fresh pike with fish-bone tongs. The fish had been caught just half an hour earlier in Lake Michigan, and it was a delicacy of the first order.

They ate slowly and said nothing for a time.

Then Herr Krug lifted a piece of pike liver up in the air and commented to Fräulein Clara Weber:

"My most gracious lady, would you be prepared to live your whole life wearing only gray clothing—with ten percent white?"

He ate his piece of pike liver, and Miss Amanda whispered very softly:

"That sounds almost like a marriage proposal."

"That's what it is!" said the architect.

Fräulein Clara said very simply:

"Yes!"

"That I find," spoke the lawyer, "to be a little hasty—and a little careless."

"Why? Why?" shouted the women.

The lawyer cleared his throat, assumed an air of importance and made the following speech:

"My ladies! You obviously do not yet understand what a marriage contract means. I know because I have led more than one hundred and fifty divorce proceedings. I know that one must not be careless in the formulation of a marriage contract. My friend Edgar is a very wealthy man. He can, therefore, afford to be a bit careless. Indeed, the lady is to be advised not to sign too quickly. First consider it! Delusion is short, regret is long."

"And your speech was also very long!" observed Herr Edgar.

"Now for my sake," spoke the lawyer, as he brought forth a fountain pen and paper, "can we get on with this. There is a case here for sure and I will earn a significant commission. It's all the same to me on which side I would be. Dear Edgar! You prefer brevity. Good! Very good! Then, a gray outfit! Velvet and silk not excluded?"

"They are excluded anyway," answered Edgar. "The clothing must be such that it does not drown out a colorful glass wall. The clothing must step aside for the architecture. Under no condition is it to compete with the architecture. Only gray fabric is allowed. That stands out brilliantly from bright colors, and provides a powerful contrast to the colorful glass architecture—and will generally be felt to be a beneficial reservation."

"To be clear," continued the lawyer, "are all tones of gray from the deepest gray to the lightest allowed?"

"Yes!" replied the architect.

"Then," continued the lawyer once again, "ten percent white should be a bit more clearly defined. Is it all the same whether the white is in the kid gloves, fur, lace, or canvas?"

"Yes!" replied the architect.

"You also reject velvet and silk in white. Is that not true?"

"Yes!" he sounded back once again. Herr Krug played nervously with the fish-bone tongs and removed another piece of pike.

"Now," continued Herr Walter Löwe, "the following issue needs to be further discussed: is the ten percent to be measured *en face* or from the side?"

Herr Krug twitched his shoulders and ate his pike.

"You are ill-tempered," observed his friend, "but things must be discussed. There is also a relevant backside to things."

The women smiled.

Herr Krug made an angry face, looked irately at Herr Löwe and said:

"You are not seeking a response, are you? You just want to make jokes. In any case, I think that at all times only ten percent white should be allowed to show. Its placement is completely up to the woman. I must not allow this subject to be discussed any further."

"Excuse me!" responded the lawyer as he quickly wrote, "then I can have the contract drawn up immediately. If something were left out, then it would only be to the advantage of your cosigning party. That seems fair to me."

The Tower of Babel rose up like a cone such that each floor was a little smaller than the one below it. Then, suddenly, from the lower floors ascended delicate violin music. And it was the melody of a waltz.

At the same moment, the light went out in the glass walls.

And the lanterns came down from the ceiling and moved up and down, and then up and down to the beat of the music.

This all looked very beautiful.

And the whole Tower of Babel shouted with many voices, "Bravo!"

And they clapped their hands.

*   *   *

After the lantern dance, the light fixtures disappeared up into the cupola and were extinguished, so that now only the table light shone in the Tower of Babel.

The four, sitting on the uppermost tower platform, ordered capon, compote, and Swedish dishes.

They drank the best Rhine wine.

And Miss Amanda spoke deliberately:

"I thought the wedding couple might now toast to close friendship."

And it was done!

And then the big spotlights shone in the glass walls so that the walls were illuminated piece by piece. The spotlight moved very slowly, perpetually changing the composition on the wall.

Miss Amanda and Mr. Walter Löwe congratulated the wedding couple.

Herr Löwe read the contract out loud.

Then they became very lively and spoke about everything possible. And they smoked.

On their second cigars, both men spotted a waiter dressed in gray at a respectful distance; Herr Krug waved for him, and he responded:

"The airship is ready to fly from the large airport on Lake Michigan."

"Then we must set off," responded Herr Krug. "I am expected. My wife's luggage can be sent along to us tomorrow."

"Where to?" asked his wife.

"To the Fiji Islands in the South Seas. I am also building there. And my workmen are having a great deal of difficulty."

Thus answered the architect.

"Indeed," shouted the lawyer, "we must seek the nearest registrar here. There is one in the building. I will summon the employees. In half an hour the whole thing can be processed."

He got up and left.

Herr Krug ordered another round of liqueurs and smoked his third cigar.

The women also smoked and discussed the exhibition. Miss Amanda, laughing heartily, told the story of Herr Krug's silver purchase and asked Frau Krug to telegraph just as soon as she could.

*   *   *

After finishing the procedure at the registrar's office, Herr Krug and his wife boarded a motorboat and proceeded to their airship. For a long time, Miss Amanda and Herr Löwe waved white handkerchiefs to the departing couple.

Shining like an opal, the glass palace lay there, mirrored in the waves of Lake Michigan. Frau Krug looked with wonder when she saw the splendid compartments of the airship's gondola: all of their walls contained glass and they had splendid balconies from which one could look out toward the earth below and to the starry sky above.

*   *   *

Herr Löwe walked back to the city with Miss Amanda Schmidt. They frequently turned around to look at the colorfully lit airport, which was situated not far away in the middle of Lake Michigan. And from there they saw Herr Edgar Krug's airship take off. They stood where they were. Herr Krug let his spotlight play in the sign language known to everyone at that time.

With his spotlight Herr Krug said:

"From my point of view, human energy seems to be underestimated."

Miss Amanda laughed, and it rang out in the balmy night air. Herr Löwe laughed just as loudly.

"I guess that's supposed to be a farewell message!" said Miss Amanda.

The lawyer, however, spoke solemnly:

"That referred to a discussion we were having before we met you, my dear lady! Edgar is very curt and often abrupt; one becomes accustomed to his ways. As a rich man he can do anything that is allowed. And one cannot argue that Edgar is unenergetic. Moreover, he is a first-rate businessman. We spoke, after all, of energy and comfort. I was in agreement with his ideas on the latter, but you should have heard all that he swirled forth. He praised the time at the beginning of our century—but with words that sounded almost like a worship of energy. How Edgar glorified the first airship flight! He knew the development of the airship perfectly; he knew the names of all those who had given their lives to airships. After having heard Edgar speak with so much excitement, one pardons some of his tartness. You surely must have wondered tonight, my dear lady, how I put up with so much from Edgar. But Edgar is an enthusiastic fanatic, and that explains everything. He who truly recognizes the energy of others and always tries to produce a greater energy in himself is not allowed a harsh word against being equally attacked or avoided."

"All that you have just told me," responded Miss Amanda, as they approached the skyscrapers of the city, "is very interesting. You have already answered a few dozen of my questions before I even posed them. Just one other question: Do you consider this marriage to be something that was arranged partly in the interest of business?"

"This question," responded Herr Löwe slowly, "is not easily answered. Your friend, Miss Clara Weber—now Frau Krug—gave me the impression of being very quick, fierce, and hot-tempered. Without a doubt, the lady is vivacious. And therefore I tried to change their minds. I did not succeed. I believe that a peaceful marriage does not come about so easily. But, business interests? What do you mean, my lady?"

Miss Amanda pulled out her cigarette case, and they both began to smoke.

"I thought," she said softly, "that one could speak of this story of the outfit with ten percent white as almost businesslike."

"Oh," responded the lawyer, "we should not make that judgment so quickly. Aesthetic considerations are not businesslike. After all, Edgar could have convinced himself of it at that very moment; he could have acted quite businesslike in the Tower of Babel. And it may not even be true. Besides, the gray cloth does not serve as an advertisement. Perhaps he just allowed himself to be carried away by his sudden, great temper. Perhaps! Then this rash marriage would in no way be for business."

"Perhaps!" said Miss Amanda.

Then they were silent for a while.

Soon they separated; Miss Amanda lived in a skyscraper-studio.

As she went up in the elevator, she repeatedly said:

"Perhaps!"

From high up, the view was spectacular; the full moon glittered on Lake Michigan.

*   *   *

Convalescence Home for Air Chauffeurs, Fiji

On one of the British Fiji Islands, Herr Krug was to build a convalescence home for elderly air chauffeurs.

It was to be erected on a rather extensive tongue of land. Twelve huge transport steamers that had carried the glass materials were still situated nearby. The steamers continued to be used for transportation purposes.

First of all, Herr Krug discovered that the spit could not be built upon. It was necessary that another, larger piece of the island be included in the building site.

"And the accommodations on the site," he continued, "although they are all of glass, are not really suited for the home of a lady. We must immediately build an extra house for my wife."

Frau Clara remained in the cabin of the airship. She soon received the following telegram from her husband:

"Dear Clara, unfortunately, I cannot ask you to come down. There is no reasonable house for you here. I have ordered that one be put together with utmost urgency. In the meantime, telegraph Miss Schmidt and send along my greetings. Also say hello to Herr Löwe. Describe the building terrain. You can see everything quite well from above. Make sure that the air conditioner is working well. You could take a leisurely trip over the Fiji Islands. See you tomorrow night. Everything will be finished here by then. Yours, Edgar."

Frau Clara placed this telegraph in a large enamel box, then telegraphed the following to Miss Amanda Schmidt:

"Dear Amanda! We landed here after four times twenty-four hours of travel. It was a wonderful trip. We ran into a hurricane over Honolulu that was not going against us. It pushed us along with such great speed that we arrived over the Fiji Islands sooner than Edgar had expected. This honeymoon will remain in my memory forever. I am not accustomed to such great luxuries. Three older women serve me alone. Edgar is below building me a house. In the meantime, I remain on the balcony of my cabin. Edgar sends his greetings to you and likewise to Herr Löwe. I cannot tell you anything more concerning the gray cloth and ten percent white. Up here I can go as I like—move, sit, and lie down as I wish. The tropical air is splendid, and the air conditioning is functioning wonderfully. The building site looks more like a desert than anything else. But twelve steamers frame the picture, and some smoke rises from them. I see an indescribable number of piles of glass—scattered around. A few walls have already been erected—colored walls, naturally. I believe this Edgar will make me completely color sick—sick for colors, that is, because I always have to wear just gray. Many iron frames can be seen below. I am curious about the workmen. They all wear white clothing. But in their profession they cannot possibly remain so clean. Below, some small glass houses are already finished. They are not good enough for me. That is why I must remain up here alone and telegraph you. I am now arranging a pleasure trip—high over the Fiji Islands. I will telegraph you again sometime during the trip. The sun is rising, and we too must rise higher. In the tropics it is really very hot—even with the air conditioner. Yours, Clara Krug."

This telegram was immediately sent down to the radio station from which it was transmitted to Lake Michigan. During her pleasure trip, Frau Clara also sent this to Miss Amanda:

"I am always telling our helmsman by telephone: 'Higher please!' 'Lower please!' 'To the right please!' 'To the left please!' and so on! And the air-vehicle travels just as I want it to. We are able to send the telegram out from another radio station. As a result, I can express myself more freely. I find the islands so beautiful that Edgar and his glass are not even necessary. Here one could practically give up all art. Smaller islands seem like colorful flower beds. And on them are huge eucalyptus trees. One sees little of the natives. They probably sleep in holes in the earth and never think about glass architecture. Please tell me what you think of the priceless marriage contract. Do you think, in a way, that Edgar married me as a sandwich lady?[2] Do you think he felt he needed one? I do not know. But I think about it all the time. He does not have to do things like this. Next we will travel to the South Pole. I mean, not over all the land, but to an area with perpetually frozen ice. Who shall I impress with my gray? I do not understand my husband at all yet. Do you think he just wants to possess me as an aesthetic contrast? Do you think that his terribly colorful world of glass is already becoming too colorful for him? Sometimes I think so. Meanwhile, after that we travel to Borneo where a giant bath will be built. Then Japan and India. The sun is going down. A tropical sun! Oh! I wish I could take a color photograph. The tropical sky is wonderfully clear. Individual stars are coming out—and the Southern Cross. I never want to stop sending you greetings. Stay well! Do not forget me! And good night! Yours, Clara."

This telegram too was rushed along. And two hours later Frau Clara was sleeping in her cabin. One could hear the rustle of the sea. A pair of seagulls flew overhead. And the servant began to heat the cabin since night in the tropics is very cold.

*   *   *

The next day Herr Edgar Krug had a great quarrel with his workmen; one of the building's owners had arrived from England and demanded that the area not be made too colorful since the eyes of the air chauffeurs were not to be too strained.

---

2. Translation of *Reklamedame;* Scheerbart's variation on *Reklamemann* or sandwich man, a man with advertising boards hung from his shoulders.

Herr Edgar now spoke most solemnly:

"I too want something simple. But simplicity can also be colorful. For centuries, old church windows have had a calming influence on human optic nerves. Why should it not be calming today?"

"Indeed," responded Mr. Webster, the English building owner, "that may be exactly right—at least in theory if not in practice. But here the air chauffeurs should have a convalescence home, and only the desires and views of these pilots are authoritative. Opinions and considerations about aesthetics are of little value here. The air chauffeurs are against the colors and want single-colored, large plates. The whole site should become unified on a grand scale."

Herr Krug said many things in an attempt to salvage the colors; he had a house manufactured for his wife in cinnabar and orange— and also built a hall in the same colors for evening dining.

The mosquito nets were then stretched open. And then came the evening with the sun far down on the horizon. Frau Clara Krug was introduced to the men, particularly to Mr. Webster, in the most solemn manner.

"You can see," said Herr Krug, "from my wife's outfit that I have a taste for simplicity. My wife always wears gray with ten percent white. The air chauffeurs will have nothing to complain of concerning me. They shall also have simplicity of color, just as they wish. I would be a bad architect if I did not consider the wishes of my clients. That is what every architect must understand first and foremost. Without a doubt, the artistic and aesthetic only come second."

Frau Krug was dressed almost exactly as she had been in Chicago five days earlier.

The most splendid orchids smelled fragrant on the dinner table.

And many fruits made the table very colorful. Herr Krug had arranged everything.

Herr Webster then said:

"When one sees this colorful table and then hears your good speech about simplicity, one becomes a bit confused. But your wife's clothing creates a delightful contrast with the colorful table."

Thus they praised the gray cloth and spoke more about the whole site. The moon came up and shone on the sea. It looked dark red through the mosquito nets.

Mr. Webster said:

"It seems to me that two colors are enough for the whole site. The orchids and the fruits are already so colorful. One must have the opposite. I would be all for dark violet and carmine."

Herr Krug looked meaningfully at his wife.

And she said:

"Cinnabar and orange could be added to those."

Mr. Webster bowed gallantly and said softly:

"If you wish, my dear lady!—Indeed!"

"Therefore we have," observed Mr. Krug, "four colors at our disposal. And thus everything must be built according to its prospective effect. The area must be closed in by hills. On these hills there could be glass windscreens in four colors. Long passageways could be fastened up there. And below are the ponds, swans, and orchids—and a pair of motorboats so that everything works smoothly. What do you think of this, Clara, my dear?"

Now, Frau Krug was in complete agreement with her husband and wanted to hear more about the whole layout of the site.

Herr Krug continued to explain his plans to her.

"Do not forget," he said nervously, "that we have a tropical climate. The sea may be seen from all the hills. The windscreens can be fastened so that the sea can be viewed frequently at the end of two screens running parallel to each other. That is very effective and also allows them to be fastened in such a way that the sea can be viewed from low down near the orchids. One makes a cut in a pair of hills, covers the groove with colored glass, and then he has the same perspective effect from the lower-lying land on which the houses should be placed."

Thus they spoke further about the rest of the site, and Mr. Webster listened more to Frau Clara than to her husband.

After a few hours, Mr. Webster was in total agreement with all of Herr Krug's plans.

The next day Herr Krug gave his workmen more precise diagrams.

And immediately various windscreens were erected. They were done only in orange, violet, carmine, and cinnabar.

Frau Clara was always with her husband and took a great interest in the work of the fitter and the glazier, and in the leisure benches.

At this time it was discussed whether the rail line was going to be laid. Mr. Webster advised against it, and Mr. Krug said laughingly:

"Thank you for that. I would like small automobiles that could be raised or lowered on elevators. But then that requires a smooth surface everywhere. In addition, we could use litters to carry people. Then the natives could also have something to do."

Then came a long discussion over the color of the tiles. Herr Webster again wanted two colors, violet and white.

Then Frau Clara was encouraged to speak her mind.

And she said:

"As far as I am concerned, there should also be black and white!"

To that, however, Herr Krug commented with wrinkled brow:

"That is indeed a little too ordinary. We will go with violet and white; that way the battle over the colors will come to an end."

Later, Herr Krug dined with his wife in the cabin of his airship high in the sky.

Frau Krug received a telegram from Miss Amanda. It said:

"Dear Clara! Many thanks for your lovely words. They do not ease my greatest worries—on the contrary. At the moment Mr. Löwe is in New York. I have sold all the pieces I exhibited. Now I think frequently of you and am concerned. Mr. Löwe also says that this cannot produce a good marriage. I am surprised that you went into this so easily. Surely you will be turned into a sandwich lady. I do not think that is so good. I would not have done it. Besides, I see the whole marriage contract as quick and, indeed, tyrannical. The man wants to show that he has power over you. I would not let that happen to me. I do not want to get agitated. In any event, I now fear that it will end in conflict. Tell me when it goes that far. Everything is going well, so I do not want to say anything. I must, naturally, ask you not to tell your husband my thoughts. Give him my greetings and many greetings to you from your Amanda. To hell with these foolish tricks!"

Frau Clara placed this telegram in the transparent enamel box where the first telegram from her husband also lay.

*   *   *

Frau Krug remained up in the cabin of her gondola for fourteen days since, down below, the metal work made too much noise. The balloon was always automatically filled. And the airship circled the building site a couple dozen times each day. Very often, Mr. Krug and Mr. Webster were up in the cabin attentively watching the progress of the metal workers and glaziers.

"Now," mentioned Mr. Krug one morning, "the most important piece of the whole site is finished. How do you like the entire site from the bird's-eye perspective, Mr. Webster? We must place extra importance on this since the air chauffeurs will usually approach their convalescence home by air. And—the first impression must also be the strongest. Now, Mr. Webster, do you like our project so far?"

Mr. Webster was quiet for a while.

Then he lit a cigar and blew the blue smoke into the morning air.

Frau Clara was still asleep and Herr Edgar said slowly and laughingly:

"The windscreens do not seem very massive from the bird's-eye view."

"No!" shouted Mr. Webster, "they certainly do not."

"We need some sort of roof!" continued Herr Edgar. "I will give my workers the order, through color signals, to attach two roofs to a screen."

"That," said Mr. Webster, "will greatly increase the value of the whole site. Glass is a very difficult material."

"You forget the lever," responded Herr Edgar; "with a lever one can not only lift the heaviest objects—but one can easily direct them."

A shrill whistle sounded from the foredeck, and the colored signals informed the workers below of what Herr Edgar wanted.

After this, another screen was placed on the windscreen in such a way that it could be adjusted upwards by counterbalance and could be fixed at any angle—and it could also touch the floor on the other side.

"In this position," said Herr Krug, "the vertically standing screen is not going to be thrown around even in the strongest hurricane, which must be a consideration; the roof screen is placed at an angle and the wind has a well-protected plane to attack."

"Wonderful! Wonderful!" shouted Mr. Webster.

When Frau Clara appeared two hours later, there were already five towering, vertical windscreens provided with roof screens—two of these roof screens were angled.

Now came more roof screens.

"Ah," shouted Mr. Webster, "you have prepared everything. Now one can approve of it. From here the hills look as though they were planted with houses. The roofs are simply striped. But there is a cupola or a bell-shaped roof. Indeed, you have prepared everything. A small surprise for me. What do you have to say, Frau Clara?"

"I am delighted!" shouted Frau Clara.

Then the men shook hands, and Herr Krug ordered a Swedish breakfast.

*   *   *

Eight days later, the whole site was complete with glass roofs. The roofs were easily set at various angles through the counterweight of the lever.

And it was for this reason that those flying in from the air always encountered a different charm. The various angles produced varied views of the roofs.

Mr. Webster was very happy with it all and expressed his happiness in long telegrams, which, through wireless telegraphs, were quickly sent to London and there made the best impression on the company of the rest home.

Mr. Krug and his wife then said good-bye to Mr. Webster and his workmen, and they celebrated the departure until the first light of morning.

Then the married couple traveled south in their airship while the sun rose in the east.

With sunrise, Herr Edgar ate fresh common crabs and drank soda water with good burgundy.

Below, Mr. Webster traveled to Borneo in the last of the twelve steamers.

The workmen got three days off.

*   *   *

On the trip south, as it grew steadily colder, Herr Krug explained various details about the site and the Fiji Islands to his wife.

First, he had to explain the lever. "Imagine a great balance," he said. "You want to lift as many hundredweights on one side as you wish. You can always lift the hundredweight high when you put exactly as much weight on the other side. This play with levers is the central element in the art of engineering. The architect always has to calculate this. It is unspeakably simple and yet so important. The biggest buildings are only made possible through levers. Of course, the lever arm must have the appropriate strength or else it breaks apart."

Herr Edgar sketched out a number of examples for his wife in which the lever played an important role.

"If the Egyptians," he added, "had understood the full significance of the lever, they would have built structures much larger than the pyramids."

"But how," Frau Clara later asked, "is the glass protected against hail?"

"It is simply wire-reinforced glass laminated together," responded Herr Edgar. "That resists the hail. Between the two sheets of glass lies a thick wire mesh and the whole thing is melted together. The mesh does not infringe too much upon the effect of the colors. It is my opinion that much more wire-reinforced glass should be used in contemporary glass architecture. Actually, the site on the Fiji Islands represents just an architecture of appearance.[3] In the end, it is indeed colorful. The principle is saved. And you helped with this. Carmine and orange were your contributions. Thank you, Clara."

He kissed his wife politely on the hand.

A thunderstorm started up, and they returned to the heated cabin.

---

3. Translation of *Scheinarchitektur.*

The sea roared violently.

Herr Edgar commanded the airship to fly higher.

And at an altitude of one thousand five hundred meters, the air was very still.

*   *   *

In New York, Herr Löwe heard more and more of Edgar Krug's buildings.

Krug's buildings on the Fiji Islands were spoken of quite frequently.

People wanted to hear details about Herr Krug's marriage. But Mr. Löwe remained silent as a grave.

Miss Amanda Schmidt also let no details escape.

Various hints appeared in the press, nonetheless, because ultimately the registrars in Chicago were not as quiet as they should have been.

But what reached the public concerning the marriage contract was a distorted picture of reality. They said that Miss Clara Krug had obliged herself once every week to wear a garment decorated with cloisonné—and the garment supposedly weighed thirty pounds.

Mr. Löwe was asked and, remaining serious, stated that nothing was allowed to be said.

Thereafter, the reporters compiled completely unbelievable nonsense about Mr. Krug.

And he heard nothing of all this. He was down south flying over the pack ice of Makartland[4] and had difficulty finding the

---

4. Makartland appears to be an invented place. It may, however, reference the Austrian artist Hans Makart (1840–1884), the "magician of colors" known for his neoclassical history paintings.

painter-colony for which he had also created glass buildings. He would build more in the region of the South Pole—but there they resisted glass and wanted buildings of wood.

*   *   *

Herr Krug had sent three of the twelve steamers from the Fiji Islands with glass material, iron, and steel-reinforced concrete plates down south to Makartland.

Then from one of these transport steamers came the following message:

"There was a huge snowstorm here. Landed in the port with a great deal of difficulty. Ice in motion. Many seals and sea lions here. The second steamer has just been sighted on the horizon. Unfortunately no news from the third. The snowstorm just started afresh. We advise turning around. The colony is not visible."

Two hours after receiving this telegram, Herr Krug and his airship also found themselves in the middle of the snowstorm. It was a great experience for Frau Clara. Herr Edgar had often experienced similar conditions, but he explained that this snowstorm was particularly terrible. He showed his wife the snow scrapers in their fiercest activity. Again and again, the scrapers flew over the hull of the ship loosening the snow.

All the cabins were heated.

Herr Krug wanted to turn around.

But this was not an option. The storm carried the balloon directly to Makartland.

And in ten hours they came to their destination. They had not been carried along as rapidly even by the hurricane that once had seized them over the Samoan Islands.

Once they were over Makartland, it became imperative for them to locate the airport. Herr Krug telegraphed to the transport steamer to make itself "heard"—since above, at the moment, they were unable to see a thing.

And then, suddenly, the people in the airship heard a pair of shots ring out in the polar night. Then they saw flares and spotlights. The steamer was discovered.

Herr Krug's helmsman thought that they might have easily come to the South Pole if the steamer had not signaled.

The landing maneuvers turned out to be unusually hard. With great difficulty, the crew let the airship be pulled down by the steamer. Meanwhile, the colony remained invisible in the continuing storm.

Shivering with cold, Frau Clara exited the body of the airship and entered the cabin of the transport steamer, where she was immediately offered hot grog. Since the crew smoked heavily, Frau Clara lit a light cigar too and drank grog—three full glasses—like an old salt.

As he entered the cabin, Herr Krug wondered more than just slightly how his wife could adjust so well to each situation. The anchoring of the airship soon proved to be almost totally impossible. They needed to let the gas out. With this, the cabin sank so deep into the snow that the whole airship was rendered as invisible as the colony.

*   *   *

The crew of the steamer was surprised that the cannon shots had been audible over the drone of the hurricane. But that could be explained by the wind's direction and the location of the balloon.

Frau Clara kept putting her hands over her ears; the sounds of the storm were still heard in the steamer cabin.

Then, with a jolt, the music of the storm stopped.

One heard only the rush of the sea. It roared violently. But it was considered a relief. The sounds of the hurricane in the sky above were much louder.

Then it was morning.

The sun was dark red over the horizon. And countless seals and sea lions tumbled around in the sea.

Frau Clara saw none of this while she slept. And Herr Edgar was very pleased that she slept. It was now time to free the balloon from the snow and to find the colony. The first activity claimed a full month, while the second lasted twenty-four hours.

The sun was still on the horizon when Herr Krug traveled with his wife in an automobile-sled to the colony. Many stars shone in the dark blue sky. The wind was completely quiet.

People from the colony drove the automobile—on a very dangerous road.

After various small accidents, they finally arrived at the colony where all comforts were available to bring the young married couple back to life.

"It was a small expedition to the South Pole even though we are still a couple hundred kilometers from the actual South Pole!"

Thus spoke Edgar Krug.

Frau Clara said laughing:

"If that was just a small expedition, then I must thank you for not continuing further. I will be happy when I am back in the tropics."

"Wait!" shouted her husband, "you do not yet know the painter-colony on Makartland. Maybe you will like it here better than you think. Besides, the repairs on our airship will take a bit of time to complete."

*   *   *

Frau Clara enjoyed herself in the painter-colony. Her husband was always out during the first weeks, working to bring the airship to the balloon hangar.

Finally, Frau Clara was once more in the company of women. These women took great pains to ensure that the famous architect's wife was happy.

Herr Krug was often in bad spirits. The airship had sustained considerable damage. And the third transport steamer had been lost and remained so.

Ten families lived on the colony.

There were twenty female painters and ten fathers who were also painters in these families. Ten of the women were unmarried daughters.

Now, they wanted to arrange a big party for Herr Krug and his wife—in the fine, heated cabin salon[5] in which all the walls were made of black wood. The women appeared in their most colorful outfits. Only Frau Krug came in a gray dress with ten percent white.

Herr Krug smiled and said:

"You see that my wife wears gray clothing with ten percent white. She represents simplicity and steps back in contrast to the glass architecture. This is certainly a surprise for the ladies."

It was indeed a very great surprise for the whole colony.

They maintained that the cabin salon certainly did not display glass architecture—and that Herr Krug loved colors so much.

Herr Krug looked at his red, partially bandaged hands, thought of his airship, and said:

"That you make do here without glass architecture—that is my deepest anguish."

---

5. Translation of *Kajütensalon*.

Then it was explained that the furnace was not functioning well. The spirit of the party was dashed to the ground when Herr Krug proceeded out with the painters, had everything explained to him, and ordered a huge repair. He also wanted to remove the more recently built cabin salon, with its wooden walls.

And when it was noted that the heating devices worked very well after the process of their repair, they cooperated with him completely on this score.

Then Frau Clara's gray outfit again made an impression, and the big club room of the colony, into which the salon cabin was built, shone as brightly as the architect had wished, with its splendid colored-glass walls.

The women of the colony all appeared in unpretentious clothing, and the party continued in the greatest comfort. Frau Clara played the harmonium, and four women performed a grand violin concert to everyone's delight. They drank hot grog and chartreuse, Benedictine and champagne. There was also beer—from Melbourne.

*   *   *

After a few weeks, Frau Clara telegraphed the following to Miss Amanda:

"Dear Amanda! A catastrophe is fortunately not yet upon us. Indeed, I must say one thing: The contract pains me. The ladies here do not ask why I always wear gray with ten percent white. One of the older women who serves me is a very talented seamstress, and she always makes my clothing varied—despite the contract clause. It is delightful how this woman always interprets the ten percent white in a new way. Now I wear a great deal of fur. One of the painters asked me about the enamel dress. Indeed, I do not understand. Hair-raising nonsense must be published in the American newspapers. Telegraph me with news of what is going on. Of course, I do not say a word about the marriage contract. I am actually ashamed that my life is bound to such a contract. But the polar nights are wonderful. And the snow is dazzlingly beautiful. We always walk with wooden sticks in front of us when we go out. God only knows why Edgar still wants to have glass architecture here. I do not know. Indeed! On this subject, he recently said that he would like to build with transparent glass, so that a peculiar effect will be made with illuminated ice flowers. One misses the flowers a lot here. There are only a few tulips and a couple of pots of snowbells. These are Edgar's favorite flowers. Telegraph soon. It is coming up to evening tea. Your old Clara."

At evening tea, Herr Edgar explained to the painters that he wanted to build them verandas with transparent glass. And that is what he did over the next few days.

Finally, the third transport ship arrived. The second was already there, having arrived shortly after the first.

Herr Krug remained at Makartland for nine months and took a great interest in polar painting.

*   *   *

Herr Krug gave the builders his plans for the expansion of the colony and had them first build a street of light towers to the balloon hangar and to the port. The individual light towers took the form of obelisks and could not be obscured or buried in a snowstorm. On top of them, moving colored spotlights shone forth.

Miss Amanda telegraphed everything she knew concerning the American papers.

Frau Clara found a friend in Käte Bandel to whom she confided everything.

Käte Bandel was unmarried and decided to join Frau Clara.

Clara was very pleased by the voluntary offer.

After three quarters of a year, when their departure was celebrated, Frau Clara complained in a lively manner about having to travel again.

And her husband said triumphantly:

"Don't you see? That is exactly what I said would happen."

It was also very sad for Käte Bandel. She would have preferred to remain on Makartland. But she did not want to leave her friend alone at any cost.

Frau Clara had no idea that Fräulein Bandel was making a great sacrifice for her.

They again saw many seals and sea lions in their furs. Then they traveled by sled through the street of light towers to the balloon hangar where they all boarded and circled Makartland three times high in the air.

Then the colonists disembarked. Still standing, they drank one more glass of hot grog—and the airship traveled north—to the tropics.

*　　　*　　　*

And soon the Australian continent lay under Herr Krug's airship.

They saw huge eucalyptus forests from the balcony of the gondola's cabin.

Herr Krug had to fly as low as possible so that the ladies could see the land as clearly as they wanted.

And they also saw a number of kangaroos. Käte Bandel made many sketches of the landscape and constantly spoke of the beauties of the colony on Makartland.

"You have taken great exception," she said to Herr Krug, "to the fact that we have built a black wooden box in the club room. As far as I am concerned, one can call it a box. We called the box our salon cabin and have passed very pleasant hours there when it was cold out or a hurricane raged. How we valued the warmth in that small room. And the black, wooden walls kept out the noise of the storm so well. I can understand that you, Herr Krug, as an architect, would always be in favor of the best and most beautiful building materials—just as with glass. However, I fear that a longing for wood in the polar area will not be overcome."

"Why?" asked Herr Krug.

"Now," replied Fräulein Bandel, "I just explained it to you: The storm does not sound so loud and one has the feeling of coziness. But you would rather build a couple dozen walls of reinforced concrete plates and say that one is able to live much more cozily in a glass palace than in a salon cabin made of wood. Surely, I think that the wooden box is the habitable box. Yes! Yes! But would it not be very friendly of you to be a little more in the polar area? The male painters already make everything you want. They are good-humored—the painters. I am afraid now that the men will build their old wooden box again or build another somewhere else. You are not returning very soon to colorful Makartland. Dear Clara, you have not yet experienced the most splendid things with us down there. The sea was always very rough. But there are times when it is very still and seems like a sheet of ice—a sheet of ice in the midnight sun when it stays close to the horizon—by the light of the full moon! It is, pardon me, Herr Krug, more beautiful than glass architecture. It is, in fact, a model for glass architecture. The smooth plane of ice is just like a smooth plane of glass. It is a shame you two did not see this. You ought to have spent more time in Makartland."

Herr Krug wanted to know more about the smooth, snowless sheet of ice.

And Fräulein Bandel explained it so vivaciously that a very excited Herr Krug suddenly sprang up and shouted to the steward:

"Quick! Two bottles of champagne—red champagne of the best stock!"

*   *   *

In the meantime, the lawyer Herr Löwe sat in his skyscraper hotel in New York and met with a Herr Stephan, who introduced himself as a filmmaker.

"I just wanted," said Mr. Stephan, "to ask a few questions concerning Mr. Krug's marriage. You were there when the marriage contract was written up. I know everything. Miss Krug must always wear black clothing. Miss Amanda Schmidt was also there. Now, I want to make a color film of the Tower of Babel—and include the supper over which the contract was settled. Very interesting! A sensation for Europeans! I'll offer you ten thousand dollars if you'll work with me. Miss Schmidt can get the same amount. Mr. Krug and his wife would be played by an actor and an actress."

"It really is a completely crazy idea," shouted Mr. Löwe. "Besides, black is not the proper color."

"Very well," said Mr. Stephan, "then we'll choose gray. It doesn't have to be so precise. The Europeans will think it's a sensation anyway. And through this they will be introduced to the glass architecture of Chicago. That is the main point! The show's direction contributes to this factor. It is, in fact, a giant advertisement."

"Then," responded Herr Löwe, "you must double the honorarium."

"More than twelve thousand dollars," shouted the businessman, "I am unable to pay. Even with good intentions. It simply will not work."

"Then pay," said the lawyer earnestly, "fifteen thousand dollars."

"Thirteen thousand!" shouted the filmmaker.

"Thirteen," said Herr Löwe, "is a bad number. Let's say fourteen!"

Mr. Stephan was scornful of this superstition, and they settled on thirteen thousand five hundred dollars.

"Wait," added Herr Löwe, "first ask Miss Amanda Schmidt. She decides. If she does not want it, then it is no deal."

"I'll go immediately to Chicago," said Mr. Stephan with his hat in his hands, "and arrange everything."

Everything was arranged after some telegrams had been exchanged between Miss Amanda and Mr. Löwe.

On the same day everything was accomplished. And a month later the film was released to the whole world.

*   *   *

When Herr Krug's airship was no longer over the Australian continent but drifting over the island of Java, the architect began to explain the Kinabalu[6] baths on Borneo to both ladies.

"You ladies," he said fiercely, "do not believe how many impossible wishes are received by an architect. It is not easy to manage rich men. One never knows whether the clients want only to do business, or if they merely seek pleasure; or if they are inclined to support aesthetic interests. My experience has been that most clients have no idea of what they really want. The architect must first suggest a couple of ideas. That's never easy—especially when it has to do with a corporation in which the most powerful figures are not recognizable as such. But it is a different story when a rich client has his own idea. Then, it is most often such an adventurous, unattainable idea

---

6. At 13,455 feet, Mount Kinabalu is the highest peak on Borneo.

that one gains an enormous respect for the rich client's flights of fancy. Please pardon me for lingering so ponderously on this introduction. But this introduction to the story of the Kinabalu baths can not be avoided. It all started five years ago. At that time the whole of Mt. Kinabalu, which lies on the northern tip of Borneo and rises 4,110 meters, was to be transformed into a pyramid. You laugh! Sure, it's easy to laugh. But I had to talk the rich client out of the idea. At first, I acted as though I accepted the idea. He wanted to create a counterpart to the Egyptian pyramids. He often said that those are pyramids of the dead, while here the giant pyramid would be for the living. So I suggested that it be a world bath with the guests of the bath staying on the mountain. 'Yes! Yes!' he thought, laughing, as he ordered the oldest Rhine wine. And then we debated the idea for several days. Finally, something reasonable emerged from what had initially sounded like a crazy idea. The mountain remained a mountain; it was not turned into a pyramid, but rather, at all levels on the mountain there arose delightful colonies and restaurants. Kinabalu lies just above the equator. Therefore it was only natural that the visitors to the baths be settled higher up on the mountain. And that also happened. Now the entire peak of the mountain has been made inhabitable. Naturally, the site will not be finished for another twenty years. But that doesn't matter. What is in place at this point can be seen. And, the Kinabalu baths are already fashionable today. I hear now that there are fifteen thousand visitors at the baths—in spite of their very considerable cost. The most important thing was negotiating the transportation of luggage and people from below to above and from above to below. Of course I suggested the cogwheel-train. But the rich client opposed it saying that the cogwheel-train did not fit an aesthetic program that utilized so much glass. And now they've built a lever-train. It is an especially fun thing. We'll land on the top of the mountain. We'll probably arrive, as my helmsman says, during the night.

You'll be astonished by the Kinabalu baths. We should be there in forty-eight hours."

The women were now very curious.

And they looked forward to the famous Kinabalu baths like children.

*   *   *

The next day, over the large island of Borneo, a couple dozen pink flamingos landed on the gondola cabin and also on the balcony, where they were fed.

Most of the animals flew off, but three flamingos remained as house pets. They were fed so lavishly by the ladies and Herr Krug that they no longer flew away.

Soon thereafter, the airship travelers saw Mount Kinabalu. Many spotlights flickered around the peak of the mountain. Herr Krug announced his arrival with spotlights—and then the airship circled the mountain, and Herr Krug's ladies saw that nearly a hundred airships and airplanes were on the mountain. They all gave greeting signals with their spotlights so that the landing appeared very festive from above.

Now the women would embark upon a great and brilliant social life. When he saw Mr. Webster, Herr Krug put the women in his care, and he immediately dedicated himself to the directors of the bath corporation. Mr. Webster showed the women everything worth seeing— particularly the lever-trains. These devices transported people and luggage up and down in a couple of minutes, using five-hundred-meter-long lever-arms. They moved very quickly, always in great arcs through the air.

*   *   *

Then the women were given days to themselves. One night at a lantern festival two thousand meters high on a sea terrace, Fräulein Bandel persuaded Frau Clara that, instead of ten percent white, she should wear ten percent plaid (very colorful, checked silk). Frau Clara agreed and did what Fräulein Bandel desired.

And in this manner they both appeared in the huge mountain restaurant.

Herr Krug happened to approach them.

His expression showed such indignation that Frau Clara, blushing, said:

"Forgive me!"

"No!" he shouted wildly.

"I made her do it!" shouted Fräulein Käte Bandel.

"Then," said Herr Krug calmly, "I recommend that you take the next airship—one leaves early tomorrow morning—back to Makartland."

"I'm going!" said Fräulein Bandel.

Frau Clara put on her coat and accompanied Fräulein Bandel.

Herr Krug took the lever-train down to the beach and, in the middle of the night, took a lukewarm bath in the waves of the ocean. The bathers below were carefully protected from sharks by nets.

Herr Krug thought his wife would accompany Fräulein Bandel all the way to Makartland. But Fräulein Bandel traveled alone.

And Frau Clara appeared again in gray and ten percent white as though nothing had happened.

Herr Krug was cool but polite, and he never again spoke of the ten percent plaid.

Frau Clara telegraphed Miss Amanda:

"You will not believe what I have experienced. It was too horrible. Edgar can really wear a cruel look. It could frighten an animal-trainer! I wore ten percent plaid. And there was Edgar's look. Miss Bandel left me immediately. Now we act as though nothing happened. But I fear that I can not endure this sort of tyranny much longer. Clara."

And Amanda telegraphed:

"I would not have tolerated such tyranny even for an hour. Amanda. Telegraph me again if anything happens."

*   *   *

One evening, the young couple met up with Mr. Webster again in one of their favorite mountain clubs, the restaurant of the White Elephant. The innkeeper, a very talkative man, told the story of the death of an old friend who had owned many tame flamingos, which had unfortunately disappeared.

Herr Krug told him about the flamingos that had come upon the airship. And it was soon quite clear that these flamingos had belonged to the deceased old friend. Mr. Krug gave the three birds as a gift to the innkeeper of the White Elephant. The animals were immediately brought around, creating a stir everywhere. As the deceased man had no next of kin, the ownership passed along without formality.

Frau Krug wanted to say something.

But her husband quickly cut her short and said:

"With this, a painful remembrance recedes quickly into the darkest background."

Mr. Webster misunderstood this and replied:

"Yes, we must still visit the back area of the pub. It is, indeed, quite worthy of being seen."

Then they saw how the splendidly colored sun set into the dark blue sea. They proceeded next to the much-vaunted rear area—to a large hall in which the walls were, of course, of glass. But here the glass was bowl- and shell-like so that the wall appeared different from each point of view. Of the shells, embedded deep in the wall, many were opalescent—and others were like Tiffany clouds—there were also some of colored ice-glass, and there was filigreed glass around the borders. Thus, from behind, the shells were variously illuminated, which gave them their enrapturing effect.

Herr Krug suggested that his wife stand at many different angles before the glass wall. He then declared that the gray cloth was the best outfit to be worn in front of the glass wall. Other women, who were nearby at that moment, agreed with the architect. Frau Clara soon found the whole thing quite embarrassing. Wanting to leave, she pretended to have a headache.

They all traveled on the lever-train to the peak of Kinabalu.

*   *   *

And from the peak of Kinabalu, they saw a wonderfully starry sky. All the stars shone very clearly against the dark celestial background.

And the stars played on the waves of the ocean, which seemed raised upon all sides like a giant shell.

A few airplanes with spotlights traveled through the night air.

It was very quiet on top of the mountain. They did not hear a sound from the breaking waves of the sea.

Frau Clara shivered, and her husband placed a large cloth around her and ordered a glass of grog.

The men then drank grog to Frau Clara's health.

They sat till midnight in the restaurant on the peak.

Only colored lanterns and the stars in the sky shone above.

The moon was not to be seen.

Meteors moved along parabolic lines across the starry skies.

On the horizon Venus was radiant.

*   *   *

The next day the Krugs traveled to Japan where they came upon a completely different glass realm lying in a small mine. Because a very comfortable temperature predominated here, all the women, and particularly the small Japanese women, went around in airy costumes that were, naturally, ablaze with very, very bright colors. Herr Krug did not like these since they overwhelmed the color of the walls.

Here too, Herr Krug wanted to praise the significance of his wife's gray clothing. He had come, however, to the wrong place. In particular, the small Japanese women opposed him.

The Marquise Fi-Boh remarked:

"My noble sir! Your comments on contrast would surely have made quite an impression in Europe—which seems so backward. What does not make an impression there? But your aesthetic holds not a syllable of truth, my noble sir! Your colorful architecture is as delightful as a sunrise over the Pacific Ocean. Your wife's outfit—and pardon my directness, my lady—is as repugnant as an old ghostly shroud. I pity your wife from my soul, my noble man! Will you allow us to change your wife's clothing?"

"No!" shouted Herr Edgar wildly.

And he grabbed Frau Clara by the arm and wanted to leave with her at once.

"What impertinence!" shouted the small Marquise Fi-Boh.

And then Frau Clara suddenly had to laugh, and all the ladies laughed too, so that it echoed shudderingly through the quiet glass rooms.

Now, in a deplorable state of mind, Mr. Krug explained that he had a headache and asked to be dismissed.

He walked silently with his wife to the nearest elevator.

*   *   *

The architect then proceeded with his arrangements there, albeit in great haste, sent his farewell card to the women and men in the community, and took off in the airship in the darkness and fog so that Frau Clara Krug could not be seen a second time in Japan wearing gray clothing with ten percent white.

The airship traveled to North India, where Mr. Krug was handling the details for an architectural site in a great zoological park.

Frau Clara telegraphed Miss Amanda from Shanghai:

"Amanda! Now the matter has become amusing. I was simply laughed out of Japan. My husband left there in fog and darkness. All the things one experiences when one wears gray with ten percent white! It is scarcely believable! I am in great suspense as to how it will unfold. Do not telegraph! Wait until I have shared more with you. The Japanese Marquise Fi-Boh had a talk with Edgar. Simply heavenly! More later! Now we are going to India. I am very cheerful and remain, as always, your old Clara."

This telegraph of course aroused a great deal of curiosity on the part of Amanda in Chicago. She shared the contents of the telegram immediately with the lawyer Walter Löwe, who was still involved with business dealings in New York, and had practically forgotten the story of the cloth.

*   *   *

Twenty miles southwest of Shanghai, Frau Clara observed from her gondola balcony that not too far away an airplane was plunging almost straight down to the ground. She shouted:

"Edgar! Edgar!"

He came, saw the aircraft, rushed back to the helmsman, and there activated a machine. Through wireless signals he maneuvered the steering mechanism of the airplane and managed to steer it sideways just before it touched the earth, allowing it to land perfectly correctly.

During this maneuver, Frau Clara became so alarmed that she had a small crying fit.

Through color signals they communicated from the airship to the fortunate airplane.

And then came the answer—also, in color signals—as follows:

"Mr. Burns here from the zoological park in North India. Many thanks for saving my life. I must have had a slight fainting spell."

Mr. Burns was brought up to the airship with his apparatus.

*   *   *

In the zoological park, which was located at the foot of the Himalayan mountains, Mr. Burns made the whole of his comfortable and spacious accommodations available to the architect and his wife.

Mr. Burns was in charge of the tame animals—particularly the goat and buffalo herds. He was an enemy of all wild animals and wanted to persuade Mr. Krug to say some strong words against feeding the tigers, lions, and leopards.

Miss Clara Krug was also supposed to work in this direction.

Mr. Krug promised to do everything possible, but at the same time he pointed out that the zoological corporation would not be able to change the entire plan of the huge site. He thought it would be something to attain gradually.

And Miss Clara stated that she had absolutely nothing to say— and that she was dependent upon her husband in all matters. This, however, came out with a strange twitch at the corner of her mouth. And the architect looked with raised eyebrows at his wife, not knowing whether this declaration of servitude was a great mockery or a nonsensical phrase.

Edgar just said softly:

"Ten percent plaid!"

Obviously, Mr. Burns did not understand and thought that his life-saver was also an enemy of wild animals—and that satisfied this ally of goats and cattle.

The site of the zoological park was so enormous that one could not view it fully from any single vantage point up in the gondola of the airship; they had erected many mountains and ravines for the animals.

This area of valleys was not visible from many points. First of all, the architect had fenced off areas for specific animals with high walls. They now stood complete, together appearing very primitive to Mr. Krug, given that they were made of brick for the most part—which was, of course, contrary to glass architecture. But there were electric carriages running over all the walls. And elevators carried the train cars up and down. And the walls had many loggias from which one could comfortably observe the animals. The so-called lion pits were particularly popular with visitors to the zoological park. More than a hundred lions bellowed on a very large piece of land. That created a very big bellow.

There was no lack of light towers and large lanterns. The whole business impressed Herr Krug very little.

"More glass!" he often said.

And then he strongly praised the view of the snow-covered mountains.

"I would like," he said to Mr. Burns, "to build on the whole mountain range. That would certainly be an exercise. Unfortunately, our time is not yet ripe for truly bold architecture."

Mr. Burns glanced askance with awe at the architect. And he avoided his lifesaver, whom he simply considered crazy. Miss Clara observed this and smiled.

There was a great area of land that one might call a recreation space, where races of horses and giraffes, elephants and mules, etc. took place. There was also a cinematic theater.

A Mr. Stephan from Chicago introduced himself to Mr. Krug and invited him and his wife to the cinema.

And this is what was playing:

"The Wedding of the Famous Architect."

Mr. Edgar and Miss Clara watched with ever-widening eyes how, in the Tower of Babel, they signed their marriage contract. The voice of the gramophone resounded energetically in the theater as Clara said:

"I am prepared to wear gray clothing for my entire life. I am do-ing this because I love glass architecture so much that I would never wish to create competition with a colorful outfit."

Thus it continued in the small theater. Miss Amanda Schmidt and Mr. Walter Löwe also spoke. And the whole presentation lasted just under half an hour. They heard the pop of champagne corks, saw the dance of the lanterns and the splendid colored-glass walls that beau-tifully surrounded the Tower of Babel.

Herr Stephan gleefully rubbed his hands. The married couple rocked back and forth in their chairs.

Herr Edgar finally stood up and wanted to leave Mr. Stephan with a short bow. He did not succeed in doing this because Miss Clara shouted at the end of the show:

"Herr Stephan, you forgot the ten percent white. Was Miss Amanda also played by an actress? She must have been a very tal-ented actress."

Mr. Stephan said, foolishly interrupting:

"Yes! Yes! A talented actress. She charged a disgustingly large fee. The story was filmed especially for Europeans. They do so like to see sensations—and particularly wedding sensations. I never heard anything about the ten percent white. Too bad! Too bad! Please, don't disclose that to anyone."

"And," observed a grim Edgar, "Mr. Löwe was also played by an actor?"

"Yes! Yes!" Mr. Stephan shouted back.

"Then you must be notified that I am going to telegraph Mr. Löwe immediately. It is indeed strange that the story would be dragged into the public without my foreknowledge. You speak about the Europeans. I would like to inform you that I am also a European. I was born in Europe and live there."

"You live in Europe?" shouted Frau Clara. "That is news to me! Where then? Everything really went so fast at our wedding, Mr. Stephan, that I had not yet found out where my husband really lives. And soon we will have been married for a year."

"Dear Clara," Mr. Edgar responded very formally, "I live on Isola Grande in Lago Maggiore—facing Brissago.[7] On the old, long lake that the Romans named Verbano. You could have found that out long ago. But now we must go to Mr. Burns. We have promised to have breakfast with him. Unfortunately, he is quite an odd man, so I can not allow myself to bring you along, Mr. Stephan. Please excuse us. Thank you very much for the theatrical show."

Mr. Stephan bowed repeatedly and said ten or twenty times rather distractedly:

"It was my pleasure! It was my pleasure!"

And then the Krugs departed.

On the wall-train that rushed past the lion pits, Mr. Edgar suddenly roared much louder than all the lions, screaming:

---

7. Brissago is a small resort town on Lago Maggiore in the canton of Ticino, Switzerland. Isola Grande appears to be a name invented by Scheerbart for a nearby island.

"By thunder! The devil struck clean!"

At this, Miss Clara was alarmed.

Then they ate breakfast in silence. They spoke no more of Mr. Burns.

*   *   *

But now the telegraph office was set in motion. Mr. Edgar Krug telegraphed Mr. Löwe in New York:

"Just saw the film story. It is hair-raising. I ask you as a lawyer to tell me what I can do about this. To hell with fame and glory. Must one allow such things to happen? Or can one, with our laws today, do something about it? Indeed, you are brilliantly played by an actor. Are you now so famous that actors can precisely imitate you? Then I feel sincerely sorry for you. I'm in the zoological park in North India. Many wild animals. I will soon become a wild animal too. Your old friend, Edgar."

This telegram seemed very amusing to Mr. Löwe, and he immediately telephoned Miss Amanda Schmidt in Chicago and said to her among other things:

"If Edgar really does not realize that we were also active participants in the film story, then we should keep this fact a secret."

Miss Amanda was completely in agreement. She had just then received a telegram from Miss Clara that ran thus:

"Amanda! What a scandal! I will never again marry a famous man. Many thanks for all famous men. They do not interest me in the least. One is compromised in the most novel manner. And Mr. Stephan simply left out the ten percent white. I look like a night owl. Do you know well the actress who portrayed you? One does not have anything to do with people who compromise them in such a way. The best thing would be if you were to come here to the zoological park. I do not know what I should do. I would most prefer a divorce. Through renown, one comes to look like a fool in the most infamous way. I am tired. I have been laughed out of the entire world. I've had enough gray cloth. Come as fast as you can. Your poor Clara."

In short, these two telegrams led Miss Amanda and Mr. Löwe to start out on the trip to India immediately, also by airship.

*   *   *

Scarcely were the Krugs out of the telegraph office, when they met Mr. Burns who had regretfully missed them for breakfast. And next to Mr. Burns stood Mr. Webster from the rest home on the Fiji Islands.

Mr. Webster wanted to go back to London. And he had already seen all the sights, including "The Wedding of the Famous Architect." And he congratulated the couple on the little joke.

"What is there to congratulate?" asked Mr. Krug. "I have informed my lawyer of the situation. He is coming here."

"Indeed," responded Mr. Webster, "I know nothing of legal matters. In principle, I stay out of the way of lawyers. No—he cannot get here so quickly. I will suggest, in any event, a small balloon trip to the mountains. Miss Burns will accompany us. There will be the five of us. Agreed?"

It was, and soon the five floated up to the mountains in an airship with special steering—they drifted over horrible valleys and over mountains with perpetual snow. They circled over the huge Gaurisankar,[8] the highest mountain in the world, which rendered Mr. Krug very talkative.

He said fiercely:

"It is indeed shocking that no one has made this single, great world of mountains inhabitable. With the state of airship travel today,

---

8. A high peak in the Himalayas, near Mount Everest on the Nepal-China border.

one could very easily take building materials up here. The lever-train from Borneo could be used as transportation. It is indeed sad that people have not yet seized upon a higher plane of building desire. There is so much unbuilt land in the world."

Mr. Burns stroked the back of his ear and gave his wife a knowing look.

And then all five looked through opera glasses in wonder at the beauty of the glacier. They were still up there as the sun set. At midnight, they landed back in the zoological park in North India.

*   *   *

Mr. Krug spent the next few days at battle with the directors of the zoological park. The men thought that the site had already cost too much. In response, Mr. Krug said:

"Certainly the site costs a lot. There are almost forty square miles of land here on which—indeed, because it cost so much—you must have particularly beautiful buildings. Foreigners come here only because of the new architecture. Do you think that the buffalo herds and lion pits attract ten people? They don't! Surely you have made your calculations without including my glass architecture. Without it, you emerge with nothing. Visitors to the baths at Kinabalu off of Borneo will come only if they find great glass architecture here. Therefore, and I am being quite modest, I suggest the roofing-over of all the enclosure walls on which automobiles and trains already travel. I conceive of the roofs as taking every possible shape—very pointed roofs, round, flat, raking, and pitched. Naturally, all out of colored glass. And everything open below. It can be realized quickly and will have a delightful effect at night from an airship. Like colorful streets of light."

There was a struggle which lasted for days.

Again and again, Mr. Krug had to make the value of advertising clear to the men on the board of directors. Mr. Webster supported him in this.

And finally it was decided to roof a quarter of the enclosure walls.

"Something at least!" said Mr. Krug. "But there is little to be seen for all that. It seems pretty much like a defeat."

After that, the places to be roofed were selected. And the bird's-eye view was accepted as the authoritative perspective.

As was agreed, Mr. Krug gave his architects the necessary instructions, and everything was done with good humor. They still wanted to arrange a big party.

Mr. Krug then thought:

"A light-and-air party would not be bad. But we want to organize it at the end of bathing season in Borneo, when everything is finished."

The architects agreed to this, and some members of the board of directors sent invitations for the light-and-air party to Borneo and Japan.

After this, the Krugs rejoined Mr. Webster and the Burnses.

These five, who traveled up to Gaurisankar, had gradually become closer friends. They dined at an enclosure-wall pub and from the loggia saw huge buffalo herds grazing freely far below.

The ladies were filled with great enthusiasm for the light festival. Mr. Burns complained of the lion pits.

*   *   *

Not a bit of news came from Mr. Löwe and Miss Amanda. Mr. Krug was then telegraphed to go to Ceylon,[9] where the International Association for Atmospheric Research planned splendid buildings.

---

9. Now Sri Lanka.

International Association for Atmospheric Research Buildings, Ceylon (Sri Lanka)

Mr. Krug went with Mr. Webster, while Miss Clara remained with the Burnses—near the big buffalo herds.

Miss Clara Krug became somewhat bored in the large animal park.

Out of boredom, she telegraphed the following to the Marquise Fi-Boh in Japan:

"Dear Frau Marquise! I recall with pleasure your brilliant speech in the shining, multicolored mine of glass. Unfortunately, we had to travel on so quickly. And now I sit here in the animal park in North India—completely alone. Soon Miss Amanda Schmidt and the lawyer Löwe will arrive. In a few weeks, there will be a huge light party high in the clouds here. The whole animal park should be lit up. The shining Bengali tigers from Bengal will appear particularly wonderful. I am especially excited about the colored lights illuminating the lions in their pits. What would animals say about the color and light effects? Would they roar even louder than they do already? Forgive me for such a silly question, but I am bored and wish that you were here. Then everything would be fantastic. It is unfortunate that it is such a long distance. Just think about this— my wedding to Edgar can be seen here in the cinema. Is that not scandalous? Oh, I would like to express myself soon. Perhaps you could telegraph me as to whether this infamous film is also playing in Japan. Edgar wants to take this to court. And I am your poor Frau Clara Krug."

*   *   *

With advantageous wind conditions, Mr. Krug traveled with Mr. Webster very rapidly to Ceylon. And there by morning sunlight, the whole site was immediately visible from the airship.

This site would consist primarily of more than sixty balloon hangars—north of Colombo[10]—in the mountains. There, several telescopes were raised high up toward the sky—very large telescopes.

The whole thing was called the "Center for Air Research."

They wanted to push out of Ceylon into a region of higher altitude. All possible airship systems needed to be utilized for this. And so it happened that special airports needed to be built for many of the systems. In the end, they needed far more than a hundred ports because airplane systems at that time were becoming more and more complicated and took up a great deal of space. Many of the hangars appeared as huge caves, which looked as though they penetrated deep into the mountain. Generally, the shape of the cupola predominated in the buildings on Ceylon—and also the open-domed hall. The Center for Air Research was in command of extraordinary resources. Therefore, Mr. Krug had little trouble and got everything approved as he wanted.

Some halls had the effect in the morning sun of huge opals—like flocks of birds of paradise, butterflies, and dragonflies—like hordes of glowworms and fireflies and trembling colored snakes.

*   *   *

The architects in the animal park wanted to give the wife of the esteemed Mr. Krug an ovation. They knew that Miss Clara was an organ player. And so a young engineer had the idea of setting up bells, kettle drums, and trombones tentatively in ten towers so that one might sit in one place and play them as an organ.

The first attempt was achieved, of course, with electric current, and Miss Clara was invited to play on this singular ten-tower organ.

---

10. The administrative capital of Sri Lanka.

And she played such that the wild animals stopped their roaring and looked in astonishment at the sky above.

The whole colony was very excited. Frau Clara played with such pleasure on the gigantic instrument that she completely forgot her boredom. That night Frau Clara received a telegram from the Marquise Fi-Boh:

"We are already in Shanghai," it said, "and we are coming with the most brilliant silk cloth. You will be amazed. Eighty-five women accompany me. The men will come later. With respectful greetings, your devoted Marquise Fi-Boh."

"They are resolute!" said Frau Clara to Miss Burns.

In two days the Japanese were in their airship over the animal park. The full moon shone brightly and Miss Amanda played on her ten-tower organ, making the air tremble. The Japanese women, their eyebrows raised high, looked quite astonished.

"Is that meant for us?" asked the Marquise telegraphically.

"Miss Clara Krug plays!" was the answer.

Then the colorful Japanese women clapped their hands, which resounded loudly through the moonlight.

And the meeting was also a great ovation for Frau Clara.

Frau Clara suddenly saw herself between countless colorful silk garments.

The most colorful pieces of silk were laid at the feet of the organ player.

She then allowed herself to dress in colors.

They dined near the buffalo herds.

Finally, Frau Clara played almost the whole night through—often it sounded suddenly like wild waltz music. And then came the dull seriousness of the drums, like a burlesque following along.

*   *   *

On Ceylon, Mr. Krug naturally heard nothing of all this. He would not be informed.

The architect spoke with the serious scientists; Japan and colorful clothing were far from his mind—as was gray cloth.

In contrast, the hangars for the airships became increasingly splendid. The mountains on the island of Ceylon were almost transformed into diamonds. To multiply the effect many times, they also incorporated countless mirrors.

Edgar telegraphed his wife:

"Ceylon will be splendid. This Center for Air Research is probably the biggest thing that glass architecture has achieved till now. It is a pleasure to be alive when clients have extra money. Remain temporarily in the animal park until Löwe and Miss Amanda arrive. Yours, Edgar."

Now, unfortunately for Edgar, there were many technical difficulties to overcome. The engineers were becoming increasingly important. They were absolutely indispensable at the huge hangar sites.

And the architect needed compromise with the engineers. That was often difficult for him. The expert was always right. And the fantastical architect often needed to curb his great building desires. Many bridge areas and arch stiffeners were not so easily achieved. The load capacity of iron scaffolding always remained a problem. And where the engineer did not want to cooperate, the architect simply had to give in.

Meanwhile, Mr. Webster traveled by motor-ship through the Red Sea past Naples to London.

*   *   *

And Mr. Löwe arrived with Miss Amanda at the animal park.

Miss Clara received them with music from twenty glass towers.

Forty-Tower-Organ Concert, India

Miss Amanda laughed when she saw her friend in colored silk. They asked after Mr. Krug and wondered what he was doing on Ceylon.

All the Japanese women had seen the cinematographic representation of the famous architect's wedding and gradually understood the story of the gray cloth. They hated the architect.

The situation made Mr. Löwe uncomfortable. And he decided suddenly to travel to Ceylon to speak personally with his friend. He telegraphed Edgar:

"Dear Edgar! I would like to speak with you in person as soon as possible. The issue is much too confusing to straighten out by telegram. That doesn't work. I am speaking very spontaneously. I ask you to give me news as to whether you can meet me on Ceylon. Your old friend, Walter Löwe."

Edgar immediately answered this telegram in the following way:

"I am now involved in the calculations of hyperbolic and parabolic curves. Completely busy up to my ears with mathematical and physics problems. You must wait. Do not come under any circumstances. I have no time. I will let you know when I breathe a little easier. Greetings to Miss Amanda and my wife. Greetings to the Burnses and yourself. I am your much plagued Edgar."

*   *   *

In the meantime, at the animal park all the roofing arrangements for the enclosure walls were being finished.

Finally they decided to have the great air-and-light party. Naturally, the architect was most respectfully invited. Edgar Krug telegraphically responded:

"Please do everything without me. I have so many conflicts to thrash out with the engineers here that, for a bit more time at least, I am not speaking with anyone. Krug."

This abrupt refusal of the invitation was received with equanimity by the architects and engineers of the animal park. They knew Mr. Krug's abrupt manner and came to terms with it.

And so the air-and-light party came to pass without Mr. Krug.

Miss Clara played on forty towers at the same time. The new organ attracted all the visitors from the baths at Borneo to the animal park.

Countless airships and airplanes floated over the whole area.

The play of light from the spotlights made a simply fantastic effect from below.

From above they saw the colorful streets of lights on the enclosure walls.

The party went on for eight nights—one after another.

And the story made a great impression all over the world.

*   *   *

On Ceylon, however, Mr. Krug became increasingly annoyed. The small hangars were partially finished and lay there like sparkling tortoises and upside-down helmets. For all that, where more glass needed to be added in large quantities, the weight of the glass was still too heavy. The free entrance of the airplanes was not allowed to be hindered by columns, and thus there were many iron frameworks standing there, and the glass coverings were not able to be attached.

Instead of glass, the engineers wanted to use a lighter material. They suggested a wire mesh with a colorful, transparent glue spread over it. Although it was easy to repair, it would not be adequately durable, according to Mr. Krug.

In addition, the walls of the hangars were supposed to hold apartments. For these, they finally had to forego the steeply rising parabolic and elliptical shapes. And the architect did not want that to happen. The clients remained convinced about the apartments in the walls because they would provide fantastic views of the splendid-colored hangar.

Mr. Krug said scornfully to his company:

"From this example, gentlemen, you should recognize once again that not everything is achievable with money. A little bit of genius is always more important, although not always available, when the money flows in streams. Therefore, I feel that money is very awkward in the river of genius. In each case, as in architecture, one continually feels that he is traveling the wrong way out of a dead-end street. Preferably, one travels to hell. Oh, indeed!"

Such an outburst of despair naturally released very mixed feelings among the listeners, who wished for Mr. Krug to leave them soon. His obstinacy often had a disturbing effect. But now, in a moment of some calm, many things seemed easily forgiven. A huge good-luck telegram from the animal park somewhat tore the architect from this situation. The telegram said in closing:

"The light party, however, came to be first rate through the playing of the forty-tower organ. If the music played by your venerable wife had not sounded so wonderful from up in the air, the party would not have become such a global event. We say thank you to our master. And also we thank your venerable wife. The architects and engineers of the animal park in North India."

This cheered Mr. Edgar up.

He immediately telegraphed his wife:

"Congratulations! Has your forty-tower organ become a global event? I will drink a couple of bottles of champagne to your health and let all the conical sections, all the ellipses, parabolas, and hyperbolas, lie on the outer edges of the world. In any event, I am very happy that you are now also introduced to the curse of fame. Comrades in suffering become closer. I hope you too will soon be saying: Fame is

uncomfortable. Then we can console each other. Greetings to everyone and a thousand times to you. Yours, Edgar."

*   *   *

Edgar's telegram had a very strange effect on Frau Clara. The Japanese ladies had just left. And the hustle and bustle of the party gradually faded away. Mr. Löwe and Miss Amanda crisscrossed the animal
park from one end to the other. Miss Clara packed all her silk clothing
and sent it in several strong crates to Isola Grande in Lago Maggiore,
where she would set up her home.

The organ player then appeared once again in gray with ten percent white.

Miss Amanda opened her eyes wide but did not say a thing.

Mr. Stephan traveled with his films to Europe after receiving verbal assurance from Mr. Löwe that the story of the ten percent white
would not be made public.

Mr. Löwe telegraphed Edgar:

"How is it going? Can I talk to you soon? I only really came here
because of you. Kindly do not forget that. A trip to India is not a trifle.
Walter Löwe."

He received no answer.

*   *   *

Mr. Edgar Krug received a visit in Ceylon. An old school friend, Mr.
Werner, arrived and wanted to go to the Aral Sea,[11] which lay far up

---

11. Located in central Asia, straddling Kazakhstan to the north and Uzbekistan to the
south.

north, east of the Caspian Sea. Mr. Werner soon saw how much Edgar suffered on Ceylon, and he convinced the architect to leave his people there and travel with him to the Aral Sea.

Edgar let himself be convinced.

On the Aral Sea, there was an experimentation station for aquatic architecture.

Over one hundred experts lived there together on a permanent basis.

And according to Mr. Werner's reports, Edgar would be received exceedingly well, since Mr. Krug's buildings awakened such lively wonder in every building circle.

Edgar quickly telegraphed to his wife:

"I am traveling north and you will hear more from me soon. As always, yours truly, Edgar."

And he set off immediately in his airship with Mr. Werner toward the north.

*   *   *

This telegram from Ceylon made Miss Clara very excited.

"What Edgar proposes," she said to Miss Amanda, "is completely indescribable. Now he goes up north and simply leaves me, without thinking about what I am supposed to do here alone. Mr. Stephan has now gone back to Europe. We stay and get bored."

"In your shoes," said Miss Amanda, "I too would go back to Europe, straight to Lago Maggiore. There you can consider in peace and quiet whether you want a divorce or not. Don't forget that we really only came to the animal park in North India because of your separation."

"Really?" shouted Miss Clara, "And then what should I do in Europe? That I would like to know."

"Play the forty-tower organ!" came the reply; "that would at least allow you to earn a living in all the larger centers of the earth, and that way you could forego being the pretend-wife of a wealthy man."

"Pretend-wife?"

So roared Miss Clara, and she shook with rage.

Shortly thereafter, Miss Clara suddenly decided to go to Ceylon to find out about Edgar's destination. Mr. Löwe and Miss Amanda went with her. And the three traveled in a large airbus to Ceylon.

In the airbus, Miss Clara commented to her friend:

"Amanda, you probably find the furnishings in this airbus quite wonderful. But to one such as I, who is accustomed to Edgar's airship, everything in this airbus is quite primitive."

Miss Amanda replied:

"Fancy that! I gather that Edgar's airship is even of less consequence to you than it is to Edgar himself."

"What?" said Frau Clara softly, "do you really mean that? Well! You must have known that very well."

On Ceylon nobody knew where Mr. Krug had gone.

Miss Clara wrung her hands and spoke with those who had last been seen with Edgar. She further inquired:

"With whom did my husband leave?"

She turned red, fearing she would hear the name of a woman uttered in this context.

But no! They simply replied:

"With Mr. Werner."

"And where did he intend to go?" she responded.

They answered:

"To the Aral Sea!"

"Thank you!" shouted Miss Clara.

And then she wanted to go to the Aral Sea.

That, however, did not happen quickly. Airships did not travel directly to the Aral Sea.

So they needed to take additional airbuses. And thus they traveled in a time-consuming, zigzag path to the distant Aral Sea.

*   *   *

The experimentation center for aquatic architecture lay in the middle of the huge Aral Sea. The harbors around the sea were not visible from the station. Mr. Krug arrived after sunset with Mr. Werner. The station looked like a colorful play of rays of light. They hung garland-like chains with colored lightbulbs from mast to mast. The chains either hung down in bows or were drawn tight. From above, this had the effect of creating a play of lines.

The station was situated on a large number of ships, big and small. These took every possible shape—mostly rectangular—but there were also round and ellipsoidal, shiplike support elements that could be tied together in completely new arrangements. And so the station could very easily assume a completely different shape. It could also be partitioned as desired.

When the architects arrived together in their airship, the station was visible as a whole. Hundreds of architects and engineers greeted Mr. Krug showing great respect. They all knew Mr. Werner, who had lived at the station for a long time.

The most important issue for the station, discussion of which was limited to architects and engineers and which therefore did not have a great deal of money at its disposal, was to investigate which building materials could withstand water the longest.

In the building of the houses above, they often used wood with clear windowpanes. Thus, only the lights in the garlands and on the masts constituted a pleasure for Mr. Krug. He spoke straightaway about the use of colored glass in building houses. They confronted him by saying that glass was a fairly heavy material that could not be used in excessively large quantities.

Still, Mr. Krug was very happy. They planned a club room with much colorful ornamental glass. And in order to acquire the best decorative windows, they established a competition. Each participant in the competition was allowed to exhibit as many decorative glass windows as he wanted. The size of the format was left to the judgment of each artist.

To be sure, this competition was very interesting for Mr. Krug. And he worked out ten entries over the next four days. And they were done in formats of various sizes.

It looked splendid when, one evening, the whole station was surrounded by glass windows.

Everyone on the floating island got in their motorboats and traveled around the island, ever awed by the shining windows lit from behind. Each person chose up to twenty windows to be considered the best—or the worst. The results would be in by sunrise. Mr. Krug did not receive even a single vote for his ten entries.

That created a great deal of astonishment.

"Okay," shouted Edgar laughing, "my glass buildings in Chicago make me one of the most famous men. And here amongst professionals my work does not receive any favorable notice at all. In any event what emerges from this is that I have not simply applauded myself. That is how it is with fame. And I am completely convinced that everything was fair play. Gradually, my reputation as a glass architect is discredited. Eventually, one sees how much value to place on fame."

Now they tried to console Edgar. Laughing softly, he fended off all consolations:

"I too believe," he said, "that my ornamental work is not very significant. In Chicago, the effect is achieved only with the enormous mass of materials. Here on a small scale I have lost it. That does not bother me so much. I am ready, in any case, to allow the victors to take part in the development of my buildings. I would like the men's addresses."

This magnanimity made a very good impression.

Then Edgar made a droll face at Mr. Werner and hesitantly said:

"You do not understand how much it has actually pleased me to lose the competition. I truly do not think that my ornaments are very exceptional. In my opinion, one never becomes famous on account of his importance. One really only becomes famous when one pushes an indubitably good thing with hellish energy. The most famous man in my humble opinion is certainly not the most important. At least, that goes for architecture. It is also a great consolation for those who do not succeed very quickly. Only those who have developed the most energy can hope for dubious fame. Besides, do you think this defeat injures me? I certainly do not think so."

Mr. Werner looked long at his old friend with amazement and said:

"There was surely some truth in your affable speech. And it was good—really good."

He shook his friend's hand.

Soon thereafter came a telegram from the Kuria Muria Islands,[12] which are situated off the east coast of Arabia.

The telegram, which was sent to the Fiji Islands and had already gone to Makartland, Borneo, the animal park in North India, and Ceylon, contained a large new commission for the architect.

---

12. Also spelled Khuriya Muriya, these are a series of five islands off the coast of Oman in the Arabian Sea. They belong to Oman; only one of the islands is inhabitable.

"There, you see," he shouted to Mr. Werner, "how luck follows me! Thus, off to the Kuria Muria Islands. Come with me. I just have to telegraph my wife. She will think I have completely forgotten her."

He sent a long telegram to Miss Clara at the animal park in North India.

And then they both departed again in the airship, having given the directors of the sea station for aquatic architecture in the Aral Sea good suggestions on how to fasten the glass windows, and having said their good-byes.

On their farewell, the floating island was illuminated with multi-colored spotlights, which shone their light upwards to the sky, straight as a dart. The colored cones of light looked fabulous from the airship above.

The airship traveled south, directing its spotlights below at forty-five-degree angles on each side.

*   *   *

While Edgar's airship sped to the Kuria Muria Islands, his telegram went to North India, and from there to Ceylon across and diagonally following the airbus that conveyed Miss Clara, Miss Amanda, and Mr. Löwe to the Aral Sea.

The telegram arrived in the station for sea architecture just as Miss Clara appeared.

The lady was very sad.

And her friend became very indignant.

Mr. Löwe complained.

And after a few days they went to Persia. And there they had to stay for a while.

And Miss Clara telegraphed from Teheran to the Kuria Muria Islands. The telegram remained, however, unanswered for days since

Mr. Krug and Mr. Werner had not yet landed. On the islands, it was feared that the two men might have had an accident, and they telegraphed these fears back to Miss Clara.

*   *   *

On the Kuria Muria Islands there lived a wealthy Chinese man named Li-Tung.

Herr Li-Tung was a very odd man. Many architects had already cursed him as a client. For quite some time Mr. Krug had adjusted to the peculiarities of rich clients and believed that he could get accustomed to even the most peculiar. One morning, he greeted Mr. Li-Tung through color signals as he circled high over the Kuria Muria Islands. Herr Li-Tung signaled back:

"It is very pleasant, Mr. Krug, that you are here already. We feared that you might have had an accident in the air. Therefore, I must telegraph your respectable wife in Teheran. I am expecting you around midnight. Please dress yourself in red silk. My servants wait for your command. Yours, Li-Tung."

Mr. Werner looked amusedly at his friend.

"This is beginning quite wonderfully," he shouted. "Edgar, you should appear in red silk. How am I to appear?"

"The servants will tell us that!" answered Herr Krug, and he looked down in awe at the territory below. There were no fields, no forests, and no grass. Colorful majolica parquet covered the ground in terraces. The terraces were connected by steps and elevators.

"With this man, I will be in agreement!" shouted Mr. Krug.

And in the evening both friends dined in red silk.

The reception came later.

*   *   *

Li-Tung had telegraphed Miss Clara in Teheran:

"Most gracious one! Have good humor! Husband is in the clouds and has been recovered. Comes down now. Travel to Shiraz.[13] Take one of my airships there. Buy a hundred pounds worth of brocade cloth in Shiraz on me—buy the best. My air chauffeurs await you in Shiraz. I greet you, my grace, with the greatest esteem and am yours, Li-Tung."

He also telegraphed his airship in Shiraz.

*   *   *

Around midnight, a hundred women of all races on earth danced a colorful serpentine dance on the rich Li-Tung's majolica parquet. The women and their colorful veils were illuminated with color from below. The floodlights radiated out of the majolica tiles. This subterranean lighting system was made possible by setting a piece of transparent glass in place of the parquet. The dance was very colorful.

Herr Li-Tung stood up from his throne, hugged Mr. Krug and Mr. Werner, and then said:

"My Kuria Muria Islands could not be colorful enough."

Mr. Krug said to them all:

"Indeed! Indeed! That is exactly how I feel!"

And then, by the colored lights of torches, Mr. Li-Tung developed his great building scheme as tea and breakfast cakes were served on the majolica parquet.

The torches burned on fairly high masts that had been erected in a couple of minutes.

"You see," said Mr. Li-Tung, "I live here like the old emperor of China who was deposed many decades ago. I live here just as the old

---

13. The capital of the south central Iranian province of Fars Osten.

emperor lived before he was deposed. I am just a little less significant than was he. Yes, indeed! Therefore, I do not tolerate any opposition. And that did not please the other architects. Hopefully, we will tolerate each other better, Mr. Krug!"

"That seems very possible to me!" he said quietly. "But now more about the building plans, your Majesty!"

"Oh, oh!" shouted Mr. Li-Tung, "You have no right to call me your Majesty, since I am still a little less significant than the old emperor of China."

Mr. Krug bowed and said quietly:

"I unfortunately did not know the old man. The old emperor has been dead a long while."

"Yes!" spoke Herr Li-Tung. "In short, these are my plans. I would like to have houses that hang on gallows. I would like to have streets of gallows. You ask why? Indeed, do you think that I want to ruin my costly majolica parquet with the houses? Besides, I want the horizontal upper arm of the gallows to be revolving."

"That is possible!" said Mr. Krug. "One lengthens the other side of the gallows' arm, puts weight on it, and uses the lengthened side as a lever rod. If the houses were small and made completely of glass, they could also be pulled to the ground, suspended higher or lower, in any case, always be turned so that the living room were in the shade. A perpetually variable architecture. I will send immediately for the workmen from the animal park in East India."

Mr. Li-Tung looked at the architect in amazement, sprang up, hugged him stormily, and shouted:

"You have completely understood me. You do not think I am crazy. Champagne! We must pledge close friendship!"

They caroused until the light of dawn.

*   *   *

When Miss Clara arrived, she found a very high-spirited party, and many exotic women—Negresses, Indians, Persians, and so on. For the most part, the English spoken sounded incomprehensible.

Miss Clara came in gray with ten percent white.

Miss Amanda had also put on gray with ten percent white.

Mr. Löwe as well.

Then the three saw Mr. Krug in green and blue silk.

That was a big surprise.

Mr. Li-Tung immediately asked the three to put on silk and brocade quickly.

"Opposition is not allowed here!" he shouted very energetically.

"Opposition is not allowed here!" shouted Mr. Krug and Mr. Werner.

The situation became very strange. Mr. Löwe grabbed his friend Edgar by both shoulders and shouted:

"Man, I do not recognize you anymore! Mr. Stephan went back to Europe. In which court of law should I press the charges?"

"Leave me alone for a bit about that!" responded Edgar.

"But it is because of this lawsuit," shouted Mr. Walter Löwe, "that I have chased you for months."

"Sir! Sir!" shouted Li-Tung, "first change your clothes. Opposition is not allowed here."

Mr. Löwe also changed his clothes.

And then everyone boozed it up again until dawn.

The ballet troupe danced to the music of five old barrel organs.

Miss Clara found this horrible and immediately said that she was accustomed to a forty-tower organ. Li-Tung immediately ordered a three-tower organ. Higher gallows-houses would later replace the towers.

The barrel organs were taken away.

The exotic women now sang to their dance.

Miss Clara said to her Edgar:

"How long do we have to stay here?"

And Edgar replied:

"We must leave with cunning."

But only after two full months when the architects and workers arrived from India and the musical instruments were in place for the three larger gallows-houses could Mr. Edgar show his friend Li-Tung a telegram that called him immediately to Babylon.

Li-Tung wanted to go with him. But Mr. Krug said that he would return as soon as possible.

And so the Krugs went with Miss Amanda and Mr. Löwe to Babylon.

Upon her departure, Miss Clara appeared on the terrace balcony of the Krug's airship, again in gray with ten percent white. Mr. Li-Tung's ballerina danced.

And the three-tower organ, which Miss Clara had often played, was played by a very talented Creole woman. She played ballet music with bells, kettledrums, and trombones.

Mr. Li-Tung fluttered his colorfully checked silk handkerchief.

And the airship took off.

*   *   *

"That was stressful!" shouted Miss Clara as the Kuria Muria Islands went out of sight.

"But it helped my cash box get back on its feet!" said Mr. Edgar.

And Mr. Löwe replied:

"You can repay me for the whole trip."

"Yes!" said Mr. Edgar.

And it was done.

Miss Amanda wanted to speak of the gray and ten percent white, but Miss Clara said vivaciously:

"Dear Amanda, I have changed my mind in various respects. We should not talk about the subject anymore. The Kuria Muria Islands formed an intermezzo in our lives. This intermezzo has ruined our stomachs. We will speak later about the color story. I will continue, in any event, with the contract for gray and ten percent white."

Mr. Edgar, smiling, made a bow and gave his wife a cigarette.

For a while, they did not come back to the question of attire.

*   *   *

Edgar left Mr. Werner back on the Kuria Muria Islands with special instructions. Besides guiding the builders, Mr. Werner's major responsibility was of a diplomatic nature.

Scarcely was the Krug's airship out of sight when Mr. Werner said in a secret audience with Li-Tung:

"Most noble Herr Li-Tung, who is only a little less significant than the old emperor of China—a fact that I will never forget—I allow myself to observe most humbly that color is always good—very good, exceptionally good. Indeed, there are various forms of colorfulness—for example, there is shining, crackling color and sleepy, melancholy color. These two types of color do not go well together. We do not, however, want to exclude any type of color from the Kuria Muria Islands. And therefore, the color compositions of the houses hanging on gallows over the majolica parquet and those of the wardrobes should be considered. The first is established already and setting the standard. The wardrobe of the ballet women changes daily, as you know. Therefore, I asked the women to cooperate so that their costumes could be more closely controlled. Later, they must coordinate with the hanging architecture."

Mr. Li-Tung did not understand this at all. It took him three hours to comprehend it clearly. Then Mr. Li-Tung said:

"Someone get the master of the ballet!"

With this issue resolved, he recognized that later, when the hanging architecture was finished, expenditure on costumes would grow enormously, and so on, and so on.

The master of the ballet said finally:

"Enormous growth is good—very good—exceptionally good! Especially for the costumes of the women who, unfortunately, cannot grow anymore. Most are already too old for that."

Among the hundred ballet women, the news elicited a storm of indignation. The women were finally appeased by the reference to the enormous growth in the consumption of the outfits if need be. They grumbled in private.

To Mr. Krug, Mr. Werner dispatched the result of his first diplomatic action. And the hanging architecture made even more progress.

They were pleased with the glass houses, which hung in the air in greater and greater numbers.

* * *

Meanwhile, the Krugs, with Miss Amanda Schmidt and Mr. Walter Löwe, promenaded on the new quays at Babylon. In ancient Babylon they had erected new majolica embankments.

An eastern business wanted to recreate the beauty of ancient Babylon as it had existed under the rule of Nebuchadrezzar.[14] In other words, to restore it.

"What a crazy idea!" said Mr. Krug.

---

14. King of Babylonia, 605–562 B.C.

But the directors of the eastern business adamantly contradicted him. They said:

"The endeavors of different humans are themselves different. Some want the old and others the new. Besides, in the land of the Euphrates and the Tigris, we have discovered and excavated so much that we could now reconstruct an epoch of Babylonian culture.

"We have persuaded many Bedouins here to figure as warriors, court officials, eunuchs, and temple servants.

"And in order to counter the addition of strangers, we have decided to make all visitors wear Babylonian clothing in the taste of the old Nebuchadrezzar, who resided here from 605 to 562 B.C."

"Does that mean," shouted Mr. Löwe, "that we have to dress and cut our hair in the Babylonian style too?"

"Certainly! Certainly!" shouted the men on the board of directors of the eastern business. "The women can remain as they are. But they are only allowed to move using litters. The women's litter carriers are waiting at your disposal. For the men we have frilled beards and wigs. We go around as Europeans because the area belongs to us."

Miss Clara laughed very loudly.

Miss Amanda smiled.

The men bowed, and Mr. Löwe said:

"Now, whoever does not enjoy this can take the Baghdad train to Constantinople. One may escape from here on that."

"In any event," observed Mr. Krug, "this is a very polite way of letting the visitor know that, above all, his visit is considered somewhat disruptive. I can adapt myself—adapt myself as always."

When the architect and the lawyer appeared in Babylonian clothing, the women on their litters wanted to laugh themselves half to death. Mr. Krug said seriously:

"Don't laugh so long! Or else we won't be allowed to take our tour of new Babylon."

"Pardon me!" shouted one of the men on the board of directors, "it is called Old Babylon."

The Krugs' long airship was situated not far away on the flowering fields.

*   *   *

Life together in this new Old Babylon developed quite differently than they had expected. A pair of costumed Bedouins behaved in such a way that they were quickly deported. The four tended to the airship.

Mr. Edgar placed large glass windows in the ancient king's barge. The one with three rudders already traveled around the old Euphrates. They were still building the others.

Edgar also placed colored lanterns on both edges of the wide processional street. But he could not achieve much more. Glass did not have much to say here. Majolica was triumphant.

On some of the palace walls, large majolica sculptural groups were also to be attached. And many Babylonian lions—coiffured to the taste of Nebuchadrezzar—were made of burnt clay. Yet, the character of the area was not very agreeable. The beginnings of things lay about everywhere. The stockpiles of materials gave the impression of disorder, and the men on the board of directors rarely appeared. One saw just four foundation stones of a temple building in which clay had been laid with Babylonian writing.

One evening, Mr. Löwe came into the little Euphrates restaurant and said laughingly to Mr. Krug and both the women:

"Children! They do not have enough money here. Therefore, the joke with the costumes. I think that we should make a break for it as soon as possible."

"Then go," said Edgar, "on the Baghdad train."

"Good," replied the lawyer, "but how is it really going with the marriage contract? I have already seen your wife in brocade. Soon she will also be dressed in the ancient Babylonian manner. Shouldn't we quickly and legally change the issue of gray and ten percent white?"

"Yes," spoke Edgar, "we want to legally strike the paragraph altogether."

Mr. Löwe amended everything in writing and the participants signed below.

"Thus it is," observed Miss Amanda, "the clothing question taken care of."

"No way!" said Miss Clara. "By my own consent, I will continue to wear gray with ten percent white."

"But Clara!" shouted Miss Schmidt quite angrily. "If your husband wishes to see you in bright colors, what then?"

"That is our concern alone!" observed Frau Krug snippily.

Miss Amanda wanted to take the Baghdad train immediately to Constantinople. It was explained to her that the sea route to New York would be much more comfortable. Then she desired to take a motorship from the Mediterranean Sea.

Mr. Löwe left the same night on the Baghdad train to Constantinople.

The last glasses were drunk in the Euphrates restaurant without wigs, only with the black, crinkled beards. The women enjoyed this cultural-historical costume affair immensely.

*   *   *

The next morning Edgar telegraphed Li-Tung:

"Dearest Friend! I see that you found your first suggestion for your majolica terraces here in Babylon. It would be nice if my glass buildings made such an exciting effect overall. In any case, I must travel to the island of Cyprus because a large seaport building with much glass is supposed to be erected there. If I cannot come back to the Kuria Muria Islands, then you must visit me on Isola Grande in Lago Maggiore. But please, not with your ballet troupe. Greetings to Mr. Werner! We send you all our greetings, and I am yours truly, Edgar Krug."

*   *   *

After this telegram, they headed west toward the island of Cyprus. They flew very high because it was so warm.

Miss Amanda Schmidt actively regretted that she no longer agreed with Miss Clara, and she spoke often of her spoon and fork handles made of silver—mostly about her artisanal silver objects. Edgar ordered a small cabinet from her for his wife's kitchen.

"My wife has not yet seen her kitchen on Isola Grande."

This Mr. Edgar said often.

And over Cyprus, he gave a small cultural-historical lecture about the island—with these words:

"The ladies should not be surprised when I give them a small lecture. I did not give one about Babylon. But now I can no longer contain all my wonderful knowledge. The ladies must consider that Cyprus was already a very famous island three thousand years before Christ. It has been suggested that Aegean peoples from Asia Minor forced their way onto the island. These people discovered copper here. From copper comes the name of the island. Around 1500 B.C., the Egyptians received their copper from Cyprus. With the copper, a Bronze Age culture arose very early on the island, which probably, with its bronze, was predominant over all the other peoples of the East. Indeed this, as far as I know, has not yet been proved. In the time of the ancient Greeks, however, the island was famous for its wine, which was stored in resined skins and tasted greatly of the resin. I have Cypriot wine in the airship. It will convince you that Cypriot wine no longer tastes of resin today."

He called the waiter.

And the waiter came.

And Miss Clara said:

"No learned man could have made a more beautiful speech than you, Edgar! Where does all the knowledge come from?"

"I was, in fact, originally an archaeologist," replied Edgar. "Indeed, I had to give the thing up because I found it too much of a strain to dig endlessly on excavations."

They toasted to the welfare of archaeology while over Cyprus and then landed in the island's big airport.

*   *   *

The airport was situated near the old city of Kition.[15] And above the central building of the circular airport, there was a large hangar-restaurant, which really just consisted of a single hemispherical dome.

Here the men from the Mediterranean Motor-ship Society were dining just as the Krugs and Miss Amanda arrived. The hangar was lit a dark violet with lilac ornaments. The women wore white with considerable green.

Once again, Miss Clara, with her gray clothing and ten percent white, made a very good effect and they wondered about her simple outfit.

Now a decision was being made concerning the whole motor-ship port. And Mr. Krug won a quick victory. He would render the form of the port with glass architecture.

---

15. Modern Citium, on the southeast coast of Cyprus near Larnaca.

"Certainly," said one of the directors, "we would like to inform the architect that we wish to avoid anything too colorful. We prefer the simple. But the simple gray outfit of his wife demonstrates to us that Mr. Krug will not introduce the tasteless, overly bright, color magic here too, in Kition, on the ancient island of Cyprus."

"Did you hear that?" said Miss Clara to Miss Amanda.

Smiling, Mr. Krug looked at his wife. And they all drank to Miss Clara's health.

"This," said Miss Clara later to her husband, "was really my first success during our very long honeymoon."

And Edgar replied:

"Strange! You are by no means now required to wear gray with ten percent white."

They stood above on the terrace of the airport and looked out over Kition to the big, old western sea into which the sun set. Behind them lay the violet-domed restaurant.

*   *   *

Mr. Krug ordered supplies for the port. The ships, as they arrived at the port, were to enter a huge realm of glass. And large glass walls were therefore fastened to all sides of the harbor. These walls had very little ornament and revealed large panes of single-colored glass.

Mr. Krug wanted to avoid blue, so he encouraged all types of greens, reds, and yellows.

"Finally," he said to his people, "it is sufficient when the whole thing has a simple effect. Always simple! Only three colors! But these in all shades. They cannot be simple enough. A lot of single-colored, wire-mesh glass is to be brought here!"

They did what he said.

The builders nodded with much pleasure.

And soon the test walls were erected—they were double walls. Electric light shone between the double walls.

"Mr. Krug," said Miss Amanda, "I do not understand you correctly here. Everything is supposed to be simple. But the thing seems very colorful to me."

"Quite right!" Edgar replied, "I also want to make everything somewhat colorful. You fail to notice just one thing: the whole will have a simple effect."

Then Mr. Krug was called to Cairo. Miss Amanda did not want to go with them, so she took the next motor-ship to New York via the Mediterranean. She said she wanted to finish up quickly the orders for her silver goods.

"Telegraph me again soon!" said Miss Amanda to Miss Clara as she sat on the ship.

The Krugs traveled soon thereafter to Cairo.

*   *   *

In Cairo, a pyramid society had been founded.

And they wanted to raise the outside world's awareness of the pyramids' appeal.

Mr. Krug suggested that they convert the Nile's ships into precious glass ships.

That was not enough for the men.

Mr. Krug also suggested that they erect small hotels on the banks of the Nile—brilliant glass hotels.

All that was deemed too expensive.

The men said that they would like to have large glass obelisks on the tops of the pyramids.

When Mr. Krug heard this, he turned completely red in the face, and he screamed with rage at the men:

"That is certainly outrageous! You want to act in such a way with the oldest building monuments that we have on earth. Do you want to mock ancient Egyptian architecture? That is what I, as an architect, should allow?"

"You are usually such an advocate of glass architecture," they said in a friendly manner. "How is it then that you suddenly want something else?"

"Gentlemen!" shouted Mr. Krug. "I am an archaeologist and have an inviolable respect for all ancient architectural monuments. Certainly, I am also a glass architect. But I would never deride the venerable ancient pyramids with glass architecture. I will immediately publish this in all the building periodicals and unite archaeologists to protect the pyramids. I herewith break all further negotiations and leave this spot. You will not see me again!"

Miss Clara looked at her husband with admiration.

And soon thereafter they flew in their airship high over the ancient Nile again toward the north.

"Are we going now," asked Miss Clara shyly, "to Lago Maggiore?"

"No," responded her husband, "we are going first to Malta, where a museum for ancient Oriental weapons is supposed to be built."

"Just for weapons?"

Thus asked Miss Clara.

"Yes," her husband replied, "they are also part of antiquity. And I hope to be able to create glass architecture there completely free of restriction. Perhaps the buildings on Malta will be even more grandiose than those in Chicago. You will see, in any case, that glass architecture is very compatible with archaeology."

"Yes," said Miss Clara brightly, "I see that. And I also feel that your position is not always an easy one. People do not want color—it is too harsh, so they say . . . And now you must always convince them to use even a couple of colors. You must seduce people into using colors. I understand that this no small task. And—the gray cloth that I wear should help persuade the client toward this. I have gradually begun to suspect the significance of the gray cloth. Have I got it right? Or am I wrong?"

"That I don't know," said Mr. Edgar, smiling, "but next I must step on the toes of those barbarians in Cairo. I would like to make a report to the building periodicals."

Miss Clara rose.

And Mr. Edgar sent a furious report to the building periodicals. The full moon shone.

Many storks floated over the airship. A stork sat near the helmsman, then, in a little while, he flew off after the other storks.

*   *   *

Mr. Krug was received with huge banquets in Malta.

Everything proceeded without difficulty.

There were very good intentions here, but, unfortunately, very little money.

Desperately, Edgar said to his wife:

"Look! I could assemble the biggest thing in the world here. The people here are excited about glass architecture. And over and over again I find that wherever on earth there is excitement there is never any money. That is a sorrow."

"But be that as it may," consoled Frau Clara, "you must build on all those sites that have enough money available."

"There can never be enough built!" shouted Mr. Edgar, and he left the room.

"There is something insatiable about my husband," Miss Clara said to her chambermaid.

And then Miss Clara wanted to discover whether her husband had also constructed many buildings earlier.

But the chambermaid could not give her any information about this because she was first employed by Mr. Krug in Chicago.

"As what?" asked Frau Krug.

"Really," replied the old lady, "as the head of the kitchen. The position has now been taken over by another woman. She is much better suited to the whole kitchen regimen."

They spoke for a long time.

They sat out on a terrace of the great Mediterranean hotel on Malta.

*   *   *

Mr. Krug now telegraphed Mr. Webster, who spent his time in London:

"Dear Herr Webster, there is supposed to be a large museum for Oriental weapons built here on Malta. I am supposed to frame it with the most beautiful glass architecture. My plans are completely finished. But I cannot carry them through because the company does not have enough money. Could you suggest someone to whom I might turn? I would be very thankful. I do not wish to travel any further without having accomplished something here. With many greetings—also from my wife—your humble Edgar Krug."

Edgar also showed the telegram to his wife, and they both waited with great anticipation for the response.

The answer said:

"Dear Sir. Who today is interested in Oriental weapons? I would recommend to the company that they sell the weapons and, without stating their intentions, use the money to make glass architecture. Later, they will find, if the architecture is excellent, a pair of lovers who will purchase the palazzi. Otherwise, unfortunately, I do not know any capitalists who would like to donate money for the maintenance of a weapons collection. Oriental weapons today have scarcely any appeal. Many greetings to you and to your wife. Webster."

The telegram was also shown to the company's directors. They explained that they were bound to a paragraph in the will that could not be easily neglected.

Edgar immediately telegraphed the wording of the will to Mr. Löwe in Chicago and asked whether the testament could be disputed.

"Indisputable!" telegraphed back Mr. Löwe quickly.

The directors would have sold the weapons collection with a great deal of pleasure. But they were not allowed to do so. Miss Clara suggested that they connect it to another inheritance, but the directors on Malta explained that they had tried to do this long ago and received disdainful responses.

With the existing money, they would only be able to fix up, if necessary, a bare brick building.

Mr. Krug pulled out his hair in desperation—he pretended to, that is. In reality he could not pull it out at all as it was very short.

*　　*　　*

Meanwhile, in Chicago, Miss Amanda Schmidt heard of Mr. Krug's difficulties on Malta.

"This is really quite outrageous," she telegraphed to Mr. Löwe, "since we consider the Krugs to be rich people, and now their wealth does not exist at all. One experiences everything. Mr. Krug gave me a princely commission for five thousand dollars worth of silver objects. Now he himself does not have enough money to build a couple of glass palaces. That is troubling. Rich people who do not have any money make me feel sorry to my soul. Everyone in the world wants to take, take, take from them. They need money just as much as the poor. A folly greater than that of money is not to be found on the planet earth. Tell me, Mr. Löwe, and excuse me for speaking so long—but don't you think that we could place the twenty-seven thousand dollars that we made with the film at Mr. Krug's disposal? The money burns in my purse."

"Then," shouted Mr. Löwe, "put the money in a bank quickly. Otherwise, you, Miss Amanda, must own powerfully big purses. Be careful with them. One can never know when one might need them. I ask you for one thing: temporary discretion! Do nothing without my consent! So that we might possibly help Mr. Krug without exposing ourselves. Are you in agreement with me on this?"

"Yes!" said Miss Amanda.

"Then," continued Löwe, "wait a little while. Do nothing! In particular, do not telegraph Miss Clara. Do you promise me?"

"Yes!" said Miss Amanda.

*   *   *

Meanwhile, Miss Clara thought very frequently about her friend Amanda, and she telegraphed her about Edgar's difficulties.

Miss Amanda telegraphed:

"Be patient. Perhaps everything will work out well in the end. I must, unfortunately, be silent. But I am still your old friend, Amanda."

"She must be silent?"

Thus Miss Clara could not comprehend anything from this telegram. She told her husband nothing of Miss Amanda.

Edgar, however, did not give up his role. He turned with great daring to Mr. Li-Tung. Then he received an answer that he had not expected, which went thus:

"Dear Edgar! What obliges you to stand up for ancient Oriental weaponry? Isn't that quite foolish today? Do you think I would squander my money on a collection of weapons? I do not think so. I would attract an infinite number of new enemies. I am already sufficiently hated for my hanging architecture. They would prefer me to hang myself here. Half of my ballet has already left. I live everyday in a different glass villa and no longer miss the ballet. You should look at the thing sometime. Mr. Werner has made the gallows-villas with absolute accuracy. One enters each house from below. That man has humor, but I have no money for Oriental weapons. If you do not visit me, then I will visit you. Greetings to your wife and yourself. I am your gallows-humorist, Li-Tung."

This telegram was also placed before the directors. Now they asked exactly what the price would be. It was calculated that a beautiful space would cost twenty-seven thousand dollars, if they threw in the money that had been set aside for the brick building.

"Twenty-seven thousand dollars!" said Miss Clara. "That does not seem like so much to me."

And she asked Fi-Boh in Tokyo if she could supply the necessary amount.

Miss Clara received the following response:

"Most precious Miss Clara! I am very sorry that I cannot help you. Indeed, perhaps your husband was right when he specified gray with ten percent white. But I find it strange that this thrift has not carried you through difficult times. Because I import extraordinary luxuries for my toilet, I am constantly in financial embarrassment. And my husband does not help me. He just laughs at me when I run out of spending money. Oh, how much I would like to help you, dear Miss Clara! Could you not give a couple of bell tower concerts? I am your poor, constantly-living-in-financial-embarrassment Marquise Fi-Boh."

Miss Clara shrugged her shoulders.

A tower-organ concert could not be arranged very quickly because Malta lacked the towers. There were towers on Sicily, which would not, however, be very easily converted for concert purposes.

"I think," she said to her husband, "you should renounce this cause now."

"No!" said Edgar hastily, "I have just now turned to Mr. Löwe."

"And," asked Miss Clara, "what did he reply?"

"'We are waiting' was the answer."

In half an hour news came from the lawyer, indicating that the money could be sent immediately.

Now, naturally, great jubilation reigned over Malta. Herr Krug and his wife were celebrated as redeemers in the Mediterranean hotel.

Mr. Krug said to his wife:

"Do you see? One should not give up too early. Everything ends much better than one thinks. Naturally, I would not be allowed to touch Mr. Li-Tung's money. And—you can be sure that trips by airship are not cheap. Löwe remains, as always, a good and helpful friend. He now has a trip around the world behind him."

"I am very happy!" said Miss Clara.

In secret she thought:

"Now we can go home soon."

But Edgar said that first he had to do something on Sardinia.

Edgar then expressed himself rather imprecisely about his building plans in Malta.

"I want the shells over one another here," he said; "the flower-petal shells should have the effect of being behind and over one another. I want to carry the giant flower-petal motif through."

"It is not yet clear to me!" said Miss Clara.

The directors of the company were very eager to know what would come from all this, so they explained that they were in agreement with everything and showed the architect boundless trust.

From Mr. Burns came the following telegram:

"Dear Mr. Krug, you have agreed with my wishes and secretly preached against the wild animals. Now the seed has grown. The lion pits are dead. All the animals have finally been destroyed. A wall fell down during a tiny earthquake, and all the wild lions broke loose, killing a hundred sheep and ten people. The lions were shot dead. The lion pits no longer exist. I have you to thank for this. And my wife and I together send our warmest thanks. And we send you both many greetings. Mr. Burns and his wife."

Miss Clara said:

"Let me reply."

And she wrote a letter. She wanted to write a letter again. She wrote that she was very pleased about the downfall of the lion pits. They had greatly disrupted her playing on the forty-tower organ. But , her husband did not consider it important.

This Miss Clara wrote to Miss Burns.

Then, after this, Miss Clara received a telegram from Käte Bandel who was still in Makartland.

"Your Indian organ playing," said Käte in closing, "resounds here in all our ears. Now you are also famous. And you will become more famous than your husband. Has he finally allowed colored clothing instead of the gray? Telegraph back. We all send our greetings to you, and I send my special greetings. Yours, Käte Bandel."

That really annoyed Miss Clara. But her anger suddenly turned around, and she thought of Miss Käte with great tenderness.

"You," she said amongst other things telegraphically, "should not make fun of the gray cloth. It is better to have a colorful house than colorful clothing. The former makes all of life colorful, while the latter only serves vanity and makes away with money that should be for building houses. Edgar was right about the gray cloth. I want to explain it to you in person. Edgar begs your pardon for the trouble over the plaid on Borneo, and we invite you to Isola Grande on Lago Maggiore. When I am at home, you should be the first visitor."

This telegram caused great joy in Makartland. And Käte Bandel replied that she would soon appear as a guest on Isola Grande.

Then Mr. Werner came from the Kuria Muria Islands and volunteered to be the master builder.

"No longer," he said, "can Mr. Li-Tung stand living in his hanging palaces. Twelve dancers still remained on the island when I left. They could be gone by now. He wanted to come to Isola Grande and spoke much about it."

Next Edgar explained his building plans on Malta to his friend.

"It is my intention," he said, "to set six to eight glass walls in the form of shells behind one another. Between these, the weapons could be placed on tables in revolving cases. When sunlight passes through the eight colored-glass walls, it will create a very complicated effect behind the eighth wall.

"The walls do not need to reach the height of the ceiling. They should have the effect of giant flower petals."

And he showed Mr. Werner the drawings. And Mr. Werner immediately began to carry out the task.

"It takes no time to lay claim to it!" he said smiling. "In any case, I am happy to be working with a firmly standing architecture and not a perpetually moving one, as on the Kuria Muria Islands."

"The whole museum," said Edgar, "should be like a towering sculptural crescent covering hilly, towering floors."

Mr. Werner said:

"It is really a very complex idea—with the eight shells behind each other. And this you have successfully achieved. Indeed—I congratulate you. Here you have clients who have faith in you."

"That's right," said Edgar bitterly, "and no money."

And then he explained about the twenty-seven thousand dollars that the lawyer Löwe had sent.

Mr. Werner was very surprised.

*   *   *

And the Krugs went to Sardinia while Mr. Werner developed the buildings with enthusiasm.

On Sardinia, the French and Chinese had laid out a large botanical garden, the largest of the day. For the past five years Mr. Krug had been building glass palaces for greenhouses.

The area consisted of ten square miles that were frequently being rebuilt. They studied the influence of the colored glass on orchids.

Mr. Krug lived here as though he were at home. He had a small automobile at his disposal and drove daily with his wife over the splendid paths covered with colorful flagstones through the gardens and hot houses. They often took long walks through the forest that lay higher up.

"It is so quiet here," observed Miss Clara one night; "why don't we get out and eat dinner up in the forest restaurant? I am both hungry and thirsty. From up there, we could see the ocean and the sunset. No one will steal the automobile here. Perpetual air travel has exhausted me greatly."

Edgar declared that dinner up there would taste excellent—especially since they needed to climb up comfortable steps for another half hour.

As they sat in front of the sea and ate very good trout, white grouse, and delicate common crabs and drank German Rhine wine, Miss Clara wanted to know why Edgar had worked with archaeological things.

"That's easily said," replied Edgar. "Put yourself in the place of those who lived three, four, and five thousand years ago. They knew five planets in the sky and the sun and the moon—those made seven stars that continually varied their position in the sky. The mystic numbers five and seven, which played such a large role in astrology, return again and again in ancient archaeological finds. With this came the zodiac—there were twelve pictures. The radius of the zodiac can be laid six times over the circumference of the circle. This six doubled makes twelve. These are the twelve double hours of the day. The trinity probably also comes from the zodiac, the three points that do not lie in a degree allow themselves to be brought in a circular line. We continually find this very simple thing in the earliest ornament. And therefore, in this very old ornamentation, we see the belief in the sky of the ancient priests. And that is why archaeology is so interesting. But I do not know whether you have understood very much of that. At home, I have a small, very old ornament collection. There I can explain everything in more detail."

"Thank you!" said Frau Clara.

And they both looked through opera glasses at the brilliant colors of the sunset and the brilliant colors of the sea which rose up like a powerful bowl-wall.

"Really jarringly colorful," said Frau Clara.

"Yes," replied her husband, "as jarringly colorful for the eyes as your forty-tower organ music was for the ears. And, indeed, everything is very comfortable when one sits further away from the color. The distance matters for both color and sound. I can imagine a concert with explosives. Shots could have a nice effect in the distance. I am, however, so taken in by color—as well as unrefined color—the so-called unrefined color—that I must hide my passion. You see, that is really the reason why I inserted the paragraph about the gray cloth. It has now been removed. But I thank you for still wearing gray. I seem less colorful that way, right? Besides, I also only wear gray clothes."

Frau Clara smiled and held her husband's hand. And he very gallantly kissed her hand.

The waiter lit the colored lanterns even though the sun was just about to set.

And then they sat and looked at the sea. "I believe," shouted Frau Clara, "our common crabs are getting cold."

At that same moment, a telegraph carrier rushed in and shouted: "A telegram for Mr. Krug!"

Mr. Krug read the telegram and sprang very excitedly from his enamel stool.

"Outrageous!" shouted the architect.

"What?" shouted Frau Clara.

And she read the following:

"Just now, here on Malta, a hair-raising robbery has occurred. Fortunately, human life was not endangered. Four huge airships landed here an hour ago. Gray fellows with ten percent white said that they wanted to see the Oriental weapon collection. They saw it, packed it up, and brought it to the airship. The work took less than a moment. Since I was shut up alone with four directors, I could not think of a means of resistance. Then the men offered their hands in a friendly way, and flew away, high up in the air, and traveled south to the hottest of Africa. There seemed to be many Negroes among them. The museum has just been finished. Tomorrow we wanted to exhibit the weapons. And suddenly today, we have a museum with no museum objects to place in it. We were robbed. None of us carried a weapon. No one had considered such an air assault. I think that someone has played a trick on us. But now good advice is expensive. I suggest that you remain on Sardinia. The gray with ten percent white implicates your wife. Malta is English. But the English government will demand a great retaining fee if the robbers need to be followed. And the directors here have no more money. Telegraph lawyer Löwe immediately. I am outraged. The museum is beautiful. And the weapons float over Africa. We were not restrained. But there was nothing we could do. Werner."

One can imagine that the telegram made a tremendous impression on the Krugs.

It was already in the middle of the night. All the stars were shining. The colorful lanterns of the automobiles were lit. And then they went quickly to the telegraph office in the botanical gardens.

There Mr. Krug telegraphed Mr. Löwe the whole night through. Miss Clara slept in a comfortable chair in the waiting room. And she slept very well. When Edgar woke his wife at the light of dawn, she said:

"I have not slept so well for a long time."

"The lion is coming!" shouted Edgar.

"What?" shouted Miss Clara. "Is there a lion pit here in the botanical garden too? In India the lion pit was eliminated. And here near the orchids are lions—Oh!"

"Clara!" screamed Edgar, "Wake up! You are still dreaming. I mean the lawyer Walter Löwe—he is coming!"

"Silly me!" said Miss Clara. "But I really dreamt of howling lions and the lawyer Löwe was below them completely covered in lion skins, and he howled too, like a lion."

"That seems uncanny to me too," said Edgar. "I telegraphed this lawyer about the attack and right away he said that he could develop a brilliant scheme to figure it out easily. But, he added, by necessity, he must go to the scene of the crime. I want to make him stay where he is; it is so beautiful in Chicago. Anyway, he is already sitting in the airship. The lion comes. I almost fear the events to come."

The next night, the story of the robbery appeared in every paper in the entire world. But the embellished fantasy of the reporters had added so much false information that the people of the world received a very strange picture of this air-fleet attack. Some of it was intentionally falsified.

During the following days, the married couple, the Krugs, sat among mountains of newspapers.

And then Miss Clara received telegrams from lawyers, all of whom wanted to be appointed to free the lady from suspicion.

"So," shouted Miss Clara, "it is as though I already sit accused! What can I do about the fact that the robbers wore gray cloth with ten percent white. Gray cloth has become very uncomfortable now."

"And I," bellowed Edgar, "curse the damned paragraph in the marriage contract. One should be very careful in the presence of a lawyer. One should not associate with lawyers. One should be wary of counting them among his friends. Lawyers only tangle us up in affairs that are embarrassing and cost money. Lawyers do business that one should not do."

"However," said Miss Clara, "you gave it properly to the lawyer. Mr. Löwe is coming in any case. He probably wants to advise me."

And forty-eight hours later Miss Clara had explanations from eighty lawyers, all of whom wanted to advise her. Now she too complained about the lawyers.

Edgar laughed so loudly that the glass walls shook.

"Now," he shouted happily, "you are truly more famous than I. I find it strange that you have been served no written charge from the English government yet. But they know that there is no money for a retaining fee in Malta. Besides, an English state prosecutor had telegraphed me that he could handle a weapons collection as easily as a bagatelle."

"I think," said Frau Clara seriously, "that it might be time to go home. I long for a quiet family life. The honeymoon has stretched out too far. Don't you think so too, Edgar?"

"No!" he said laconically. "Besides, we have to wait patiently for events to unfold. We have fallen into a pretty story. Now while it is hot, eat up the soup. You should not have so lightheartedly agreed to the frivolous paragraph."

"That," replied Frau Clara, "is exactly what the lawyer Löwe told me."

"Indeed!" shouted Edgar. "Lawyers are always right about these things. To the devil with the whole legal system. Oh!"

He gesticulated with clenched fists in the air.

Mr. Webster telegraphed Miss Clara:

"My greatest sympathies, dear Lady. I am humbly yours, Webster."

"He did not send greetings to me?"

So asked Mr. Edgar. And Miss Clara said laconically, "No!"

The Marquise Fi-Boh telegraphed from Tokyo:

"My poor Frau Clara! You are indeed quite lamentable. You have been compromised before the whole world. And now you are implicated in a veritable story of robbery. That is very romantic indeed. But just think, the prisons of the human nations are not yet colorful glass palaces. I believe, in any case, that you must be prepared for the worst that may come from the terrible gray cloth. I am glad that I never undertook to wear gray cloth. It cannot get colorful enough for me. Telegraph me if you find yourself in prison on remand. It is indeed all very romantic. But I am happy that I have not experienced such things myself. Heartfelt sympathies, Frau Clara! Do not cry! It will not get better that way. I am yours, Marquise Fi-Boh."

*   *   *

The poor Mr. Werner did not have an easy time on Malta either. He telegraphed Mr. Edgar:

"The story has become so unbearable that I act as though I were sick. Three doctors are taking care of me. Is Mr. Löwe not there yet? The only hope! In great desperation, your old friend, Werner."

But Löwe floated over the Atlantic in an airbus. And he could not go further because of adverse storms. After a few days, he suggested that the airbus make an intermediate stop in Bermuda. From there, Löwe telegraphed Edgar of his hopes of arriving soon.

*   *   *

Miss Burns also sent Miss Clara a sympathetic telegram replete with melancholy. Miss Clara laughed for half an hour without stopping. But Miss Käte Bandel telegraphed:

"Do not despair! I will go to prison with you. It will become a prison of the merry. I send my greetings and am already at Borneo. I am here for you now and forever. Yours, Käte Bandel."

"People have all gone crazy!" Miss Clara finally said, sighing. After these words, however, she received a telegram from Miss Amanda Schmidt in Chicago with this wording:

"Now I can no longer remain silent. I supplied information for the Chicago Tower of Babel film and received an honorarium of $13,500 for it. Löwe receive the same amount. We have put this money into the museum administration in Malta. I do not want to have it back. Forgive your poor Amanda. Heartfelt greetings to you both. Miss Schmidt."

Miss Clara showed this to her husband.

He slowly lit a cigarette and looked out over the sea.

"Indelicate!" said Miss Clara softly. "But in the end she has made up for everything. I consider this Mr. Löwe a dangerous man."

Immediately thereafter, the Krugs were brought a card, on which was printed:

Walter Löwe, Lawyer

Chicago

Malta

*   *   *

In twenty-four hours Mr. Löwe had won back the Krug's trust.

He said finally:

"You cannot argue with or blame me for making an advertisement for you, dear Edgar. Women understand everything in a very sentimental way. One does no business with sentimentality. I did not simply give you $13,500 as a present like Miss Amanda. The money allowed me to take part in the board of directors of the museum administration on Malta and ensure that it becomes a museum to the history of glass architecture. In eight days the museum will open. Now the whole world speaks of Malta. One should notice that an American lawyer is on the board of directors."

Mr. Krug had to admit that this adaptation of the embarrassing situation would not undermine his efforts. The men shook hands, and Mr. Löwe left for Malta. Miss Clara had retired, letting it be known that she had a headache.

*   *   *

The Krugs lived in a townhouse within the botanical gardens. This small hotel was situated in a valley among the mountains. The colors of the glass walls shone simply with carmine and blue.

Miss Clara appeared at dinner with radiant eyes and said:

"I heard that Mr. Löwe went to Malta. I can now breathe easier, and I feel quite well."

"Me too!" replied Edgar.

After the meal, they went by automobile to the Orchid Hotel. It was situated close to the sea and had beautiful terraces.

"Don't you have a wish?" asked Edgar.

"Yes," responded Clara, "I would like to eat oysters."

"Of course, we could do that," replied the architect, "but I thought you would express architectural desires."

He ordered oysters and, with them, red champagne.

"The business with Löwe," he continued, "has developed well. He is introducing a museum on the history of glass architecture and is bringing respectability back to the plundered island of Malta. Therefore, I feel that we can go home soon. But there will be an extra salon built onto the house for you. That's why I asked you about your wishes."

"Yes," replied Miss Clara blushing, "then perhaps it could be in all gray tones, with some white and some black. Would that be all right?"

"I have glass walls in gray on Lago Maggiore," said Edgar, "but there is some gold too. White and black are not available."

"I am also happy with gold," replied Miss Clara again.

"Yes," thought the architect now, "the room is not that large and there is a harmonium in it. When you play, one hears it best in the large dining room. While playing you cannot be seen at all from the deep-set room. You can also read and write there. You will like it. I will send off a telegram now so that it will be ready by the time we arrive."

"Oh," shouted Frau Clara, "that is indeed wonderful."

She drank to him.

And then she said:

"One is not allowed to say 'thank you' for that."

Edgar laughed and gave the waiter the telegram.

"Have you received newspapers and telegrams today?" he asked.

"A small hand wagon brought them to me," she replied, "but I have not read any. I gave them all to my chambermaid."

Many large airships presently flew overhead along with numerous airplanes coming from Spain.

"They are going," said Mr. Krug, "to Malta."

"Oh," shouted Miss Clara, "now we don't want to worry ourselves anymore over the crazy robbery story. Let the world think what it will. I have nothing to do with it. Isn't that true?"

"No, you don't, dear Clara," said the architect. "But don't forget that Löwe still seems to be my friend. He made something out of the most embarrassing situation."

"Nevertheless," said Frau Clara, "these lawyers, with their business of money, are a little embarrassing to me. I judge only based on my emotions. He caused us embarrassment with the wedding contract. He earned a good deal of money from the film and was silent to us about it for months. Combined with that, he sailed around the world at your expense and became a board member of the museum's administration. I fear that he might bring us further embarrassment."

"You do not suspect," responded Edgar, "that I have already been in the most embarrassing situation? If I had not received so much money from Li-Tung, we could not be sitting here so freely on the Sardinian coast in the Orchid Hotel. And besides, they want to celebrate an Orchid Festival here for your sake. It should begin on Sunday and last for more than eight days. We must, therefore, remain here fourteen more days. You should play Bach."

"I would be very happy to do that!" responded Miss Clara.

And they ate oysters and drank red champagne.

The large sun set into the blue sea.

And many white seagulls flew over the beach.
Great airships and airplanes floated in the sky above.
"Are they all going to Malta?" Miss Clara asked.
"Clara, that I don't know," replied her husband.

*   *   *

At the orchid festival, it was specified that the women would wear opal jewelry in their hair—and gray clothing with ten percent white.

The directorship of the botanical gardens on Sardinia wanted this to serve as an ovation to the much-beleaguered Miss Clara. They felt it simply laughable that someone had wished to connect Miss Clara with the air robbery on Malta.

Meanwhile, Miss Käte Bandel arrived in Locarno and telegraphed Miss Clara to that effect. The telegram came just before the organ concert. And Mr. Krug invited the lady to come to their castle on Isola Grande. The porter was informed that the owner of the castle and his wife would arrive soon by airship. Mr. Krug communicated to the porter that he should have three rooms prepared for Miss Bandel—the most colorful rooms.

Then came the concert. And Miss Clara played old Bach very clearly and cheerfully. In thanks, the organ player was brought the most beautiful orchids—blooming in pots—under glass so they could be forwarded on immediately.

At the great dinner, Mr. Krug spoke with the ladies of the directorship.

"It must, indeed, be really excruciating," said one woman, "to travel over a large brick city."

"That," replied Mr. Krug, "I never do. My air chauffeur zealously studies the maps in order to avoid all brick sites along the way. Therefore, my airship very often takes large detours so that I will not be reminded that people are still housed between bricks. I also do not like to hear about the residents of brick houses. My dear lady, you must believe that I am very unsympathetic to brick culture. It pains me that architects today still build with bricks. No, these architects can no longer gain any respect."

Miss Clara gave her husband a telegram from Miss Amanda Schmidt who, with the articles of silver, had also arrived in Locarno.

Mr. Edgar telegraphed instructions on her behalf like those he had telegraphed for Miss Käte.

Then the two ladies sat in the Krugs' castle and waited.

"They will have good conversations!" said Miss Clara.

*   *   *

Mr. Li-Tung sat in one of his hanging-glass villas and ate breakfast. He speared a roll with an ancient Oriental dagger and smiling, brought it to his mouth.

Then he wanted to write a telegram. He had his fountain pen brought to him and saw that the ink was dry.

"In the tropics," he said gloomily, "the best discoveries dry up, particularly on the Kuria Muria Islands. I myself am drying up. By the beard of the prophet, in any case, that must be avoided. I will write with my pencil."

And he wrote the following for his telegraph office:

"Most noble and venerable architect! You, my dear Edgar! You are, as I read in the evening papers, not yet at home. You remain in Sardinia. Mr. Löwe, whom I have indeed met, has set up a museum for the history of glass architecture. You are, surely, the triumphant man of the day. Good health to he who has friends as good as yours! Be happy that the Oriental weapons were stolen. I congratulate you! I congratulate you from the bottom of my heart and soul. Soon I will call on you at Isola Grande. I send both of you my greetings and am yours. Your friendly, good, guardian spirit, Mr. Li-Tung."

He gave the telegram to a pitch-black servant, took the dagger in his hand, raised it high, and let it sparkle in the tropical sun.

*   *   *

Mr. Li-Tung's telegram arrived in Sardinia when they were having refreshments on the terrace of the Orchid Hotel. The Krugs laughed so hard that they had to explain their laughter.

More good-luck telegrams came during the next day. Mr. Webster, who stayed on the Fiji Islands, said monstrously polite words and asked for his apologies to be accepted a thousand times. Mr. Burns spoke again about the dead lions and maintained that everything should work out for the best for a lion killer.

Mr. Werner, likewise, congratulated him.

Then Mr. Krug sent Mr. Löwe a very friendly telegram. And the Krugs finally went to Lago Maggiore. Miss Clara looked constantly toward the north and could not sleep because of her yearning.

"You cannot imagine," she said to her husband as they sat on the balcony of the airship and she gazed quietly at the moon, "how much I long for quiet domesticity, and how happy I am about my gray room in which the harmonium is placed. Yes!"

She still had the opal jewelry in her hair.

Below, the Mediterranean Sea sparkled in the moonlight.

And many falling stars shone in the sky above.

It was a very quiet night.

The airship traveled with the wind and the propellers did not move.

*   *   *

Mr. Stephan sat with his film in Geneva and became annoyed.

He had made a bad business deal and was annoyed with everything.

He was also annoyed with Mr. Löwe who, with his—Mr. Stephan's—money, was making all the best business deals on Malta.

And Mr. Stephan thought about how he might have been able to photograph the air robbers.

He would have liked all too much to film the story of the air robbery.

"How," he asked himself, "should I start the story? I need a rich man who has four of his own airships. And with these we could film the story on the island of Malta. Where is this man? Ha! I know. Mr. Li-Tung has at least four of his own airships. He can make me very happy. Off to the telegraph office."

And he telegraphed everything about the great air robbery on Malta to the Kuria Muria Islands. And then he boldly offered to lease the four airships and a hundred servants.

He received the following response:

"You are certainly a very respectable man! My good sir, give me the pleasure of waiting a bit. I will soon be coming to Switzerland and will visit you there. You should meet me. Do you also have Oriental weapons in Geneva? Otherwise, I can bring some with me. Wait a little while. Then the rest will happen. I am most humbly yours, Mr. Li-Tung. Till now, still on the tropical Kuria Muria Islands."

Mr. Stephan hit himself on the forehead.

But he did not understand the telegram.

"It is probably best," he said at last, "for me to greet these unintelligible words with silence. Silence is golden."

He went around his house shaking his head while thinking about it.

"Now will he? Or won't he?"

Thus shouted Mr. Stephan.

An old German asked Mr. Stephan how one reached the top of Mont Blanc most quickly.

"With an airplane!" said Mr. Stephan.

*   *   *

Miss Clara saw her so-called domesticity for the first time. The whole of Isola Grande was a big castle with many terraces and several strange towers, many brightly colored balustrades and brightly colored walls.

Edgar had it arranged so that his airship arrived after sunset. The palace shone brilliantly. All the electric lights were thrown on with a jolt, and the towers sent spotlights off to the sides and above.

Miss Amanda Schmidt and Miss Käte Bandel greeted the lady of the house as though nothing had occurred. Both ladies were a little restrained on account of Mr. Edgar.

"I have not thanked you at all for the $13,500," said Mr. Edgar to Miss Amanda. "It will happen herewith. I will, as soon as I can, return the compliment."

He kissed Miss Schmidt's hand quite gallantly along with that of Miss Bandel, to whom he said:

"We do not want to speak anymore of the plaid folly in Borneo. I thank you for forgiving me."

And Miss Clara added to this:

"My husband has such an inconsiderate, progressive nature that one must forgive his stubbornness. He is really consistent like a true hero in a novel. The name Edgar sounds too fitting for a novel."

"Oh!" shouted her husband, "precisely because it sounds so much like a novel do I go to a lot of trouble to veil what is like a novel in me."

"Oh, yes," then shouted Miss Amanda, "with your wife's gray cloth, isn't that true?"

There was then a very funny conversation, and during supper everything was so lively that Miss Clara completely forgot to take a walk through the shining palace halls.

It was late in the night before they went to the rooms of the kitchen where Miss Amanda had stacked her silver objects illuminated by celebratory candlelight. It seemed like the giving of presents at Christmas.

*   *   *

The next day a telegram arrived from Mr. Li-Tung in Malta.

"Most noble friend," said Mr. Li-Tung, "the museum for the history of glass architecture is indeed quite wonderful here. Surely one can go further in this world with a friend as true as this lawyer, Mr. Löwe. I have pledged close friendship with both him and Mr. Werner. I congratulate you on your friends and will ensure that I am beneficial and useful to you. Day after tomorrow I will be at Isola Grande and with you again. Your very noble friend, Li-Tung."

Laughing, Edgar gave the telegram to the ladies, who became extremely curious about the visit.

During the afternoon, Edgar traveled with the three ladies in great arcs around Mount Blanc.

Night fell, and Edgar saw that Mont Blanc was completely illuminated with light towers.

"It really is completely new," he said, "what can happen when one is away from home for two or three years. One does not recognize one's home anymore. The light towers, which I once recommended for the airships, are now made by others. Now—it pleases me that my ideas have been recognized as correct."

"Are you not a little jealous," asked Miss Amanda, "that you were not consulted on the construction of the light towers?"

"But I cannot build everything!" replied Mr. Krug. "I am happy if glass architecture presses forward victoriously. I myself want . . ."

He became silent.

Miss Clara asked:

"What do you want?"

"It makes me happy," said her husband, "that the light towers look so wonderful. I want to congratulate the tower keepers."

And the spotlight sent signals from the airship in the night air. And from the towers came spotlights back, thanking the architect with both politeness and a splendid play of lights.

*   *   *

Shortly thereafter, Li-Tung arrived with four airships.

"My great client!" said Mr. Edgar to the three ladies. "One must let much happen. To entertain this group of servants will really be arduous."

But Mr. Li-Tung shouted upon arriving:

"Have no fear, my noble friend, my ships are filled with servants and architects who are here to study the beauties of Switzerland."

"Listen," replied Edgar, "that should be: 'with architects and servants.' You should not name the servants before the architects. I would hope not. In my large dining room we can all eat breakfast together. My wife will play her small organ."

And in half an hour Miss Clara played in her gray room with ten percent gold for the first time. Here, the varied gray tones of the glass had a delicate effect. The company below was waited upon by Mr. Li-Tung's servants. After the organ playing, he sought a private conversation with Mr. Krug.

And then the wealthy Chinese man said:

"Friend! I have acted in your interest. I robbed the Oriental weapons museum. Are you perhaps angry about that? Mr. Löwe helped you out of the affair very nicely. You will be soundly famous. Do you also know that fame needs to be revitalized? Oh yes, do you see? That's why I took care of it. Revitalization is important. Otherwise, fame goes sour."

"Listen, Li-Tung," replied Edgar while he sat down on a stool, "you have done a most dangerous thing. Have you told this to Löwe? What did he say?"

"He is also completely speechless," replied Mr. Li-Tung. "He said that I should confer with you."

Mr. Edgar pulled out his hair and asked for some time to think.

And then he went to Miss Clara in the gray room and explained to her what had happened.

Miss Clara said smiling:

"Just as I thought. And the lawyer is again involved. I advise, since the story is a joke, that you let it be known as such. And that Mr. Li-Tung build a museum for ancient Oriental weapons near Gibraltar. Mr. Werner can build it. And Mr. Li-Tung can transport the pieces there."

*   *   *

Mr. Li-Tung was in complete agreement with Miss Clara's suggestion.

Mr. Löwe was informed immediately.

And Mr. Werner went to Gibraltar.

The four airships left that same evening and retrieved the stolen weapons from inner Africa.

The architects, whom Mr. Li-Tung brought with him, kept busy for the most part in Switzerland with the study of the light towers.

Meanwhile, the press was informed.

And they complained very loudly about the pranks of rich men.

Mr. Li-Tung was treated very lightly. They explained in the press that his robber-like assault was a good joke that had won Mr. Krug much repute.

And Mr. Li-Tung laughed a great deal.

Mr. Krug laughed just as much with the three ladies. Really, no one could be offended by the rich man.

*   *   *

Not many good-luck telegrams arrived at Isola Grande during this time. People of the day preferred to reckon with the bad rather than the good in humanity.

From Mr. Löwe came the following:

"Dear Edgar! Do not wonder whether it seems as though I had played a hand in the denouement of the robbery story. Actually, it only appears that way. Here, the pyramid administration in Cairo, which you so grimly scolded, was accused of the deed. The people in Cairo were very much infuriated. And Mr. Li-Tung heard that. Since it was suspected that the men in Cairo were allowed to be severely wronged, Mr. Li-Tung made a serious face and said that he did not want anyone harmed. And he opened his heart to Mr. Werner and me. So that's the state of affairs. I think it speaks for the goodness of Mr. Li-Tung. Many greetings to your household and to you. Yours, Walter Löwe."

When Frau Clara saw the telegram, she shook her head and asked Mr. Li-Tung if he had behaved this way.

He admitted it in short, and asked for Mr. Stephan.

Mr. Stephan received this telegram:

"My venerable man! Now we will soon have you. Stay in Geneva. You should be picked up. Li-Tung."

The businessman had read all about the fun in Malta and thought now that a joke would be played on him.

Then, Mr. Li-Tung studied the furnishings on Isola Grande with enormous enthusiasm.

"Next, show me your workroom," he said to Mr. Edgar. "It must be very interesting."

"And it is too!" replied Edgar as he showed him a dozen spaces in which he took care of work.

These spaces were not exactly large. A few had views out over Lago Maggiore. Others, by contrast, had no view at all. They had three to four meters of reinforced-concrete walls below, with the light entering above through glass windows that went up to fifteen meters, while the small floor space was covered with a thick monochromatic cloth. Most of the time, wax candles burned in these rooms. Edgar frequently read and smoked there.

At night, they usually drove around the lake in a motorboat, and ate dinner outside or in the colorful gondola cabin. Mr. Li-Tung behaved very politely to the women, particularly to Miss Käte Bandel.

"It is remarkable," he once said to her, "that our architect has only sealed walls in his own house. It is very healthy when one sits completely enclosed by walls and is not aware of the outside world through the exceedingly close glass windows."

"I find the wall covering of the darker room very interesting," replied Miss Käte. "Especially the dark linoleum with niello-like painted ornament on the walls. I also like embroidered silk on the walls. Fur I like less on the walls. The colorful hummingbird feathers are also interesting on the solid wall.

"And I like very much the colorful majolica on the walls. I am only surprised by the fierce rejection of wood, which is so obstinately avoided in the furniture. The stone mosaic work and enamel ornament on metal are also beautiful."

Meanwhile, it grew dark on the long lake, and the many light towers on Isola Grande lit up with a jolt—and at the same time garlands of lights were illuminated which connected the towers to one another in splendid bows.

From below, the tower capitals looked very splendid. And the spotlights shone straight up out of the capitals, capping their width on all sides, high up like fantastic flowers of light.

Mr. Krug invited his guests to eat dinner outside on a large terrace. One could hardly see the stars since so much light floated and swung in the air.

And the light played over the stone parquet which was richly worked with inlay.

*   *   *

They also went over to Isola Bella.[16]

And Mr. Edgar laughingly suggested that he probably wanted to establish a competition between Isola Bella and his Isola Grande.

"I have nearly renounced flora," he said. "Architecture, in my opinion, is not kind to the plant world. The architect should also not put up with gravel paths. We have so many stimulations on Isola Bella that I in no way claim to have given something better to my island."

---

16. Considered the most important of the four tiny Borromean Islands in Lago Maggiore. It boasts a seventeenth-century chateau and terraced gardens.

"And indeed," said Miss Clara, "tomorrow we will receive the orchids from Sardinia. Oh! They are even more beautiful than glass architecture."

Edgar lit a cigar on Isola Bella, and said:

"That is for certain. Besides, they have probably already landed at the house—the beautiful orchids—truly—I am no competition for the orchids. Most surely not—nature, or the planet earth—which probably means the same thing to us—is always more wonderful than the somewhat weak fantasies of the small human, even in the best of circumstances."

"You are too fiercely modest," shouted Li-Tung. "One does not quite believe you."

"Then we shall go home immediately," replied Edgar violently, "so that we can marvel at the orchids in the blue flower-house. There we can decide whether I worked too fiercely in modesty."

And on Isola Grande they were so pleased with the orchids that Li-Tung took everything back.

*   *   *

One day, Mr. Li-Tung came to Mr. Krug and said in a very loud voice:

"Venerated friend! I believe that soon I will have stayed long enough with you. I am preparing for my departure. My airship will be here within six days. We must, therefore, thoroughly enjoy these days to the fullest. I suggest that you drive us in your airship for three days and three nights through the Alps to Tyrol and then by another route back to Geneva. Don't laugh, because I speak both of airship travel and routes. That is just the power of habit. In Geneva, we will pick up Mr. Stephan. And then he must film here for the last three days. You will allow me to let my servants prepare everything, won't you?"

Mr. Edgar hesitated to answer, but finally said:

"Yes, then we should get the ladies."

At that moment, the ladies were sitting before a balustrade on the shore, feeding the swans.

Miss Clara said:

"Indeed, one feels more at home in one's airship than in one's own home. What a pity! In an earlier time there were homemaking women. They do not exist anymore."

Miss Amanda said:

"Yes, who can own so much so as to always sit at home? One must do one's business. But, therefore, women too must have much to do. In ten days I want to be at the World's Fair on Lüneburg Heath."[17]

And Miss Käte spoke:

"I would like to travel around the world in an airship. There cannot be enough movement in this world for me."

"And not enough color," added Mr. Li-Tung. "True, don't you think, my dear?"

"Indeed!" replied Miss Käte.

The motorboat landed, bringing the packages from Locarno. And the swans swam slowly out into the lake.

Edgar had sent for books that weighed, all told, four thousand pounds.

*   *   *

Then the two men and three women traveled in the airship over the high mountains with the wind in a northeasterly direction. On Ortles,[18] situated at three thousand meters, they saw the glacier observation

17. Located near Hannover, Germany, and the site of Expo 2000.
18. The highest peak of the Italian mountain range of the same name in the eastern Alps.

station, from which, during the night, the glaciers were illuminated with spotlights.

Krug was known there and was welcomed in a very friendly way with grog and salmon trout.

Because of the great cold, they had braced the veranda with five-layered glass walls. The ladies drank tea and felt as cozy as if they were at home. North of Innsbruck were the five light towers with chimes. These towers were played from Innsbruck itself—just as Miss Clara played the forty-tower organ in the animal park in North India.

Miss Clara also played here.

And the music resounded wonderfully through the mountain world. Here, they had only large and small bells, no drums or trombones.

At Lake Chiem,[19] they visited several sanatoria that were all built completely out of glass. Here they praised the beauty of glass so fervently that Mr. Krug looked astonished. He had become completely unaccustomed to hearing praise.

In Lucerne, they stopped at the floating restaurants and attended the light shows over Lake Lucerne.

"In contrast," said Li-Tung, "are the arts of fireworks, which are nothing compared with what they had one hundred years ago."

He won one hundred pounds on a bet. The women were the jury.

And it had seemed strange that they would bet on the light show. They bet on which light-show compositions would be awarded first, second, and third prizes. The spotlights came from the mountains, from balloons, and from the surface of the lake. The women of the

---

19. The largest lake in Bavaria; is was the site of some of the first experiments with zeppelin technology.

jury were in ever-different locations, once in the air, another time on the water, or on the mountains.

Mr. Li-Tung asked telegraphically in Geneva whether Mr. Stephan was at home. And since this was the case, he urged them all to depart. He did it very quickly.

*   *   *

In Geneva, Mr. Li-Tung said to the filmmaker Mr. Stephan:

"Pack up all of your equipment—gramophone and photographic materials. We have much to do. We'll travel next to Isola Grande."

"And the attack on the island of Malta?" asked Mr. Stephan. "What about that? Is it still going to happen now that it is no longer charged with mystery? The joke of a rich man—nothing more. Everything solved. But I will perhaps do it anyway. It will just be very short now."

"Just come with me!" said Mr. Li-Tung.

The ladies opened their eyes wide in surprise when they saw the notorious filmmaker.

"Should another wedding be filmed?" said Miss Amanda softly to both of the other ladies. "Hmm! Do you think that I should be married against my will?"

"We don't think that!" said Miss Käte smiling. "But I am, in fact, curious as to what will happen."

Then Edgar came up to them and said mysteriously:

"I really don't know what Li-Tung intends to do now. I fear that something like an attack is planned again. I am, in any case, prepared for the worst."

"One should not just watch out for the lawyers," said Miss Clara. "One should also watch out for the rich men. I will remain, in any event, quietly at home for a year."

"Me too!" said Edgar, and he wanted to kiss his wife's hand but was hindered by his air chauffeur who hastily informed him:

"Mr. Li-Tung wants us drape the airship in garlands. Are we directed to do that for him?"

"Beware!" shouted Edgar. "Li-Tung, what do you intend to do?"

"Will you not allow it?" asked the Chinese man.

"No!" said Edgar indignantly.

"Good!" replied the Chinese man. "Then I shall command my servants to throw the purchased flowers out the cabin windows, individually in a great arc."

It was done.

Edgar remained silent.

The women shouted with delight:

"Oh!"

"Oh!"

"The beautiful flowers!"

And in the afternoon, they arrived at Isola Grande. And then Mr. Krug saw that his whole castle had been decorated from top to bottom with garlands of flowers and fir boughs.

He frowned, but had to admit that it looked very beautiful.

As he appeared to be satisfied, the women were too.

Li-Tung smiled.

"Forgive me!" he said to Edgar.

*   *   *

In the castle, Edgar said hastily to his wife:

"This matter has gone too far for me! I am annoyed that I gave him permission to decorate the house. I did not think that he would muck up all the architecture."

"Now be calm!" Clara replied. "We will get over this. I just don't know where it is leading."

They ate lunch in the large dining hall.

Mr. Stephan sat ready to film in one of the many wall niches.

Mr. Li-Tung knocked his Persian dagger on his glass of Rhine wine three times and said:

"This is the sign to begin filming. Now, will those present have the goodness to behave as naturally as one does in the theater."

They laughed and spooned the tortoise soup. Edgar said:

"Green growing swags hang over our dinner table. The table has also not experienced that before."

"Do not talk too much," said the Chinese man; "it costs money. I ask quickly and purposefully Fräulein Käte Bandel: Do you want, my grace, to become my wife?"

"No!" shouted Miss Käte.

"That's brave!" shouted Miss Amanda.

Mr. Li-Tung asked again:

"You really don't want to?"

"No!" shouted Miss Käte again. "One does not propose to a lady so unceremoniously."

Mr. Li-Tung knocked the Persian dagger against his glass of Rhine wine six times and sadly said:

"The ladies and gentlemen may behave as they please, and say what they want. Temporarily, the filming will not continue."

"Too bad!" shouted Miss Käte.

Mr. Li-Tung opened his eyes wide.

Outside they heard the whirring of airplane propellers. A man landed in the airport unannounced. They took no further notice of the unknown visitor.

Dinner proceeded fairly quietly.

Then they drank coffee on a beautiful terrace in front of a splendid, colorful glass wall that gleamed like silk.

Mr. Stephan appeared again with his equipment in the background.

The evening sun shone off the stone-tile mosaic.

Mr. Li-Tung again knocked his dagger on the water glass three times and spoke briskly:

"Dear Miss Bandel! Please kindly excuse me for being so curt in daring you to accept a so-called marriage proposal. But I wanted to imitate Mr. Edgar."

"A so-called marriage proposal!" shouted Miss Käte. "Sir, you go too far!"

"Look, Clara," shouted Miss Amanda, "she is aggressive. No one will speak to her about a gray cloth with ten percent white."

"I put on today," said Miss Clara, "probably ten percent garnet instead of ten percent white."

"I ask you not to take too long," said Li-Tung, "since I myself would like to speak longer. You cannot forget that the film is a very expensive pleasure."

"Stinginess at a wedding film!" shouted Miss Käte. "That is not inviting."

"By the beard of the prophet," shouted the Chinese man, "I am no miser! I swear to you that I am very fond of you. I just don't know how to find the correct words yet. Would you not like the same things as I? I will happily travel with you around the world, and there would not be any difficult paragraphs in the marriage contract. Just say yes!"

"OK!" shouted Miss Käte.

"Hurrah!" shouted Mr. Li-Tung.

They congratulated the pair.

And then Mr. Löwe appeared on the terrace.

"Löwe must always be around!" whispered Miss Amanda.

Miss Clara said:

"Then the event indeed had a purpose."

The contract was drawn up immediately by Mr. Löwe and signed.

The champagne flowed in streams.

And Mr. Stephan shouted:

"Should I, then, continue filming?"

Then Miss Käte Li-Tung said to the filmmaker:

"Now let it be; otherwise, the story really will cost too much."

*   *   *

Mr. Stephan received his fee.

Mr. Löwe also received his.

No one said anymore about the attack in Malta or even about the weapons museum in Gibraltar, which was supposed to provide competition for the Alhambra.

Later, Mr. Li-Tung traveled west with his wife, over Madeira, Isla Grande de Tierra del Fuego, and Makartland; they wanted to go to Australia. There, Miss Käte wanted to sketch kangaroos. Mr. Löwe went to Paris; Mr. Stephan, back to Geneva.

Miss Amanda went to the World's Fair in Lüneburg Heath.

And Mr. Krug had the Chinese man's flowers removed from the castle quickly.

And Miss Clara said:

"It is good that they are gone."

*   *   *

Mr. Krug also showed his wife his small museum of ornaments.

Here, steel cabinets were situated in the center. Walls and domes sparkled with blue, red, and yellow dice ornament.

"The small museum," Edgar explained, "is just a little contribution to numerical mysticism. I already indicated to you on Sardinia how meaningful are three, five, and seven. Everything goes back to the stars. The ancient priests in Babylon and other places looked more at the sky than others."

And he spoke much more about this. He also said that the seven colors of the rainbow were really not seven colors. The number seven was introduced because of the five planets plus the sun and the moon. The seven days of the week could credit their inception to the astral bodies. In music too, five and seven played important roles, and so on.

"Couldn't you go back to archaeology?" asked Miss Clara.

"No," replied the architect, "one who is seized by glass architecture lives in the glass colors. But in these, ornament is naturally the main thing. Only on account of the numerical symbolism are we impressed by antique carpets. They seem somehow sacred. But, therefore, I will not neglect my small ornament museum."

*   *   *

On the dinner table lay a telegram from Mr. Werner, who was completely enraptured by the ornament of the ancient Alhambra and spoke only of this—so much so that Mr. Krug said:

"I fear that this enthusiast could build the Alhambra again. Fortunately, he is bound to the glass in his weapons museum."

*   *   *

Miss Clara often went to the small orchid room where she cared for the delicate flowers with great zeal. She did nothing that the gardener had not stated was good.

The emerald room which shone with amethyst ornament was Miss Clara's favorite haunt. Here too there were only blooming orchids. Because of the orchids, she completely forgot her organ playing.

*   *   *

Mr. Webster telegraphed from the Fiji Islands:

"The site here, esteemed Mr. Krug, has now developed so far that all the old civil servants in England want something similar to what the air chauffeurs have. The negotiations have been so successful thus far that I will certainly be able to submit the details to you in two months. I will inform you of this: only you are being considered for the undertaking. With the utmost respect, I am humbly yours, Webster."

This was very pleasant for the architect, and he asked his wife to travel with him to Venice—in the airship.

Miss Clara happily agreed. She did not yet know Venice.

"You must become familiar," said Edgar, "with the stone parquet on Piazza San Marco. There you will observe that today we are further along than they were four hundred years ago. Perhaps, however, you will not think this, and that would also seem correct to me."

They went there.

And Miss Clara said:

"I am not yet learned enough to criticize the ornament. But you should build a second Venice nearby for the civil servants in England."

"Yes," replied Edgar, "but we must not think so often in terms of competition. That often leads to the unoriginal. I will think about it, however."

*   *   *

Edgar Krug's Model Room, Lago Maggiore, Switzerland

On Isola Grande, there arrived guests who wanted to become clients. The Krugs had to return from Venice.

Mr. Krug immediately took his guests into the model room.

There, the dome, ceiling, and walls were made rather simply— mostly just in two colors of glass.

And the individual models were situated between screen walls of gray cloth. The screen walls, two or three meters high, were able to be placed where one wanted.

There was a model castle that on first impression seemed like a heap of colored-glass balls. Each model could be turned, or turned automatically, and was able to be moved either up or down to the floor.

There were also models of very small villas in the hall, and sites with small colonies.

The visitors inevitably had very good intentions when they had very little money. And when they had a great deal of money at their disposal, they were very demanding and often wanted to have the impossible built.

Miss Clara had taken very little notice of these model rooms. Then she had much of it explained to her and soon understood which efforts were hidden in these experiments. She began to photograph them and soon had a series of images for each model.

A telegram arrived from Mr. Burns in Ceylon, saying:

"Dear Herr Krug! I am, by chance, here at the Center for Air Research near Colombo on the island of Ceylon. They are very upset that so much money was lost on the airport. They want the money at their disposal to fund air research, and all other luxuries are forbidden. I am sharing this with you so you can be prepared. They are constructing large high-altitude balloons with enclosable gondolas. They want to go up more than ten thousand meters. I fear that most of your beautiful glass halls, which shine like huge mysterious mountain eyes, were not permitted to be finished. There are so many scientists gathered here that all artistic components are pushed to the background. Many air greetings. Thankfully yours, Burns."

"Now you see," said Edgar to his wife, "how easily the best intentions can become the worst. I will be careful to console myself that, fortunately, the opposite is also true."

*   *   *

One morning the Krugs stood high up on the highest tower on the island, one hundred meters above the surface of the water.

Edgar said to his wife:

"I would like to prepare a small happy thing for you. But it is not yet ready. The money is too tight. I would like to have a bell-tower organ made for you on which you can play, so that the huge mountains roar and the surface of the water trembles. Missing are the glass towers in the mountains; thus, the bells cannot yet be put in place. Perhaps it will work with three towers."

"Yes," said Miss Clara, "but I do not know whether money should be spent on such a thing. We could go back to the animal park in North India. There, towers, bells, drums, and trombones exist in great numbers. I should also add that I did not find playing to be adequately enjoyable. For the present, we should leave the event in North India. I am now happy with the organ in my gray room."

"I wanted to make a little advertising attraction for Isola Grande," said Edgar dejectedly.

"Is that so necessary?" asked Frau Clara.

"Yes," said Edgar, "people are working against me in so many places that I must cast Isola Grande in the best light."

"Then we must ensure," said Miss Clara, "that we make do without mountain organs."

The Gray Cloth and Ten Percent White

*   *   *

On the breakfast table, Miss Clara found a telegram from Miss Käte Li-Tung.

It went so:

"My dearest Clara! Greetings. We are still on the island of Madeira. We travel with leisure. But then, we have the time. Besides, the wine here is absolutely wonderful. We have been on twenty of the Canary Islands. There are so many canaries. I have sent a dozen to you. They will probably arrive in a couple of weeks. We do not know when we will be back on the Kuria Muria Islands. My husband wants to set up a huge kettledrum organ in the sea. A couple hundred large and small floating balloons would be anchored on the surface. And one could play drums and kettledrums with a wireless. Would you be so kind as to consecrate the new instrument? You do not have to answer immediately. Think about it for a couple of weeks. Soon we shall go to Isla Grande de Tierra del Fuego, and then to Makartland. I hope that things are going as well for everyone as they are for us. Therefore, we send our greetings to you both many thousand times, and I am your old Käte Li-Tung."

"The Käte-drum!" shouted Miss Clara.

And Edgar smiled benignly as he read the telegram and said:

"There, two who belong together have found each other. I do not believe anymore that opposite personalities attract. On the contrary. The reserved want the reserved, the happy want the happy, but the sad never want the sad, or maybe they do?"

"To Li-Tung's health!" said Miss Clara, and she drank a whole glass of red wine.

*   *   *

In the afternoon, the Krugs traveled around Lago Maggiore.

And in the evening, they sat in their tower salon and ate artichokes.

This tower salon was sixty-five meters high.

Here, the architect had made a pointed tower out of the dome. The floor, covered by thick gray cloth, took up scarcely fifty square meters.

But the view from the central table up at the peak of the dome was the best Isola Grande could offer.

With their heads on the upper cushion of the leather seat, both looked up and saw the colors red, blue, green, white, violet—and so on, floating in the splendor of the peak.

"Yes, the colors!" said Mr. Edgar.

And suddenly at that moment, the afternoon sun shone through the glass top of the tower—and it sparkled and glowed.

"Yes, the sun!" said Miss Clara.

As it grew dark, the servant brought a telegram from Miss Amanda.

The servant lit a wax candle.

And Miss Clara read:

"Dear Clara! Please tell your husband that he completely forgot to send architectural models to the World's Fair. These models are lacking. Many greetings to you both. Amanda."

Edgar called his head valet, an old man who took care of packages.

The head valet was instructed to send ten models to the World's Fair in Lüneburg Heath. Edgar then gave him the numbers of the models.

Then the light, electric of course, was sent clear up to the top of the tower.

Edgar smoked another cigarette and stared up into the colorful top of the tower with his head leaning on the cushion.

"Dragonfly wings!" he said quietly. "Birds of paradise, fireflies, lightfish, orchids, muscles, pearls, diamonds, and so on, and so on— All that is beautiful on the face of the earth. And we find it all again in glass architecture. It is the culmination—a cultural peak!"

Then they ate roasted snails.

They drank fresh beer from nearby Brissago.

And then they both smoked good, Cuban cigars and, again with their heads leaning back, looked up—into the dome of the tower.

The End!

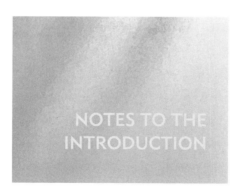

NOTES TO THE
INTRODUCTION

1. Walter Gropius in a letter to Hermann Finsterlin, April 17, 1919. Quoted in Marcel Franciscono, *Walter Gropius and the Creation of the Bauhaus in Weimar: The Ideas and Artistic Theories of Its Founding* (Urbana: University of Illinois Press, 1971), 124 n. 93. Unless otherwise noted, all translations are my own. I have translated all titles of books and articles that appear in the text into English, with original titles confined to the notes.

2. Paul Scheerbart, *Das graue Tuch und zehn Prozent Weiß. Ein Damen Roman* (Munich and Berlin: Georg Müller, 1914). References to *The Gray Cloth* correspond to the text in this edition.

3. Gershom Scholem, *Walter Benjamin. Die Geschichte einer Freundschaft* (Walter Benjamin: The history of a friendship) (Frankfurt am Main: Suhrkamp, 1975), 258. (Benjamin is not specifically referring to *The Gray Cloth* here.) Mechthild Rausch points out the limits of this comparison and states that "unlike Brecht, Scheerbart wishes to express not only his distance from reality but also the inexpressibility of his utopia." See Paul Scheerbart, *Das graue Tuch und zehn Prozent Weiß. Ein Damen Roman*, ed. with an afterword by Mechthild Rausch (Munich: edition text + kritik, 1986), 162.

4. First published as Paul Scheerbart, *Glasarchitektur* (Glass architecture) (Berlin: Verlag Der Sturm, 1914), the work has been reprinted in German and translated into English in *Glass Architecture by Paul Scheerbart and Alpine Architecture by Bruno Taut*, ed. Dennis Sharp, trans. James Palmes and Shirley Palmer (New York: Praeger, 1972).

5. In a letter written by Anna Scheerbart to Ida Dehmel on the day of Paul's death, he is described as suffering from a "short indisposition." See Mechthild Rausch, ed., *70 Trillionen Weltgrüsse. Paul Scheerbart. Eine Biographie in Briefen 1889–1915* (Seventy trillion world greetings: Paul Scheerbart: A biography in letters, 1889–1915) (Berlin: Argon, 1991), 478. There is no known evidence to support the legend that Scheerbart starved himself to death in protest against the war. It may be attributed to Walter Mehring and can be found in Else Harke's afterword to *Paul Scheerbart: Dichterische Hauptwerke* (Paul Scheerbart: Primary written work), ed. Hellmut Draws-Tychsen (Stuttgart: Henry Goverts Verlag, 1962), which was reprinted in Berni Loerwald and Michael M. Schardt, eds., *Über Paul Scheerbart I: 100 Jahre Scheerbart-Rezeption* (About Paul Scheerbart I: 100 years of Scheerbart's reception) (Paderborn: Igel Verlag, 1992), 35. I am grateful to Mechthild Rausch for bringing this reference to my attention.

6. The particulars of Scheerbart's early years are found in Mechthild Rausch's biography, the most complete account of Scheerbart's early life. See Rausch,

Von Danzig ins Weltall. Paul Scheerbarts Anfangsjahre 1863–1895 (From Gdansk into the universe: Paul Scheerbart's early years, 1863–1895) (Munich: edition text + kritik, 1997).

7. Ibid., 27.

8. Ibid., 67.

9. This famous watering hole, located on Wilhelmstraße in Berlin, was also frequented by the Swedish playwright and novelist Johan August Strindberg and the Norwegian painter Edvard Munch. See Carl Ludwig Schleich, *Besonnte Vergangenheit. Lebenserinnerungen, 1859–1919* (Sensible past: Life remembrances, 1859–1919) (Berlin: Ernst Rowohlt, 1922), 328–331.

10. Scheerbart published nine articles in the first volume of *Der Sturm* in 1910–1911 alone. The journal's book publishing arm, Verlag Der Sturm, would ultimately publish Paul Scheerbart's *Glasarchitektur*. Verlag Der Sturm ceased publication in 1932.

11. The group was included in a photographic postcard depicting "The Modern," reproduced in Rausch, ed., *70 Trillionen Weltgrüsse*, 291. The term *Stammtisch* literally refers to "a table for regulars" but is commonly used to suggest a German literary circle that grew out of the regular meetings of its members in a favored café.

12. Rausch, ed., *70 Trillionen Weltgrüsse*, 455–457.

13. From Scheerbart's autobiography of July 6, 1904, reprinted in Kurt Lubasch and Alfred Richard Meyer, eds., *Paul Scheerbart—Bibliographie mit einer Autobiographie des Dichters* (Paul Scheerbart—Bibliography with an autobiography of the writer) (Berlin: private printing, 1930), 15. The word *quantity* is the translation of *Massenhaftei*, which implicates mass media and mass production.

14. Scheerbart, *Glasarchitektur,* chapters 1, 111.

15. Ibid., chapters 26, 50.

16. Hermann Muthesius, *Style-Architecture and Building-Art: Transformations of Architecture in the Nineteenth Century and Its Present Condition*, introduced and translated by Stanford Anderson (Santa Monica, CA: Getty Center for the History of Art and the Humanities, 1994), 74.

17. Dirk Kocks argues for Muthesius's great interest in this pavilion in his essay "Deneken, Muthesius und die Farbeschau" (Deneken, Muthesius, and the color pavilion), in Angelika Thiekötter, ed., *Der westdeutsche Impuls 1900–1914. Kunst und Umweltgestaltung im Industriegebiet: Die Deutsche Werkbund-Ausstellung Cöln 1914* (The west German impulse, 1900–1914: Art and the environment of production in the field of industry: The German Werkbund Exhibition, Cologne 1914) (Cologne: Kölnischer Kunstverein, 1984), 205–221. This is the most recent of the very few attempts by scholars to deal with this work. An excellent source on the interior of the pavilion and its didactic program is found in a contemporary article by Friedrich Deneken, a contributor to its design: "Der Werkbund und die Farbe" (The Werkbund and color), in *Illustrierte Zeitung, Der deutsche Werkbund* (Illustrated newspaper, the German Werkbund) (1914), 17–18.

18. See Kocks, "Deneken," 211. The German design on display was an attempt to usurp the monopoly on fashion held by the French at the time.

19. Scheerbart, *Glasarchitektur*, chapter 13.

20. Paul Scheerbart, letter to Richard Dehmel, January 9, 1914, in Rausch, ed., *70 Trillionen Weltgrüsse*, 458–459.

21. "Even in Scheerbart's 'glass architecture' (1914)," Benjamin writes, glass as a building material "appears in utopian contexts." Walter Benjamin, "Paris, Capital of the Nineteenth Century," in *Reflections*, trans. Edmund Jephcott (New York: Schocken Books, 1978), 147.

22. Reyner Banham, *Theory and Design in the First Machine Age* (London: Architectural Press, 1960), 267.

23. Paul Scheerbart, "Das Glashaus. Ein Vorbericht" (The Glass House: A preliminary report), *Berliner Tageblatt und Handels Zeitung* (Berlin Daily News and Trade Newspaper) 537/42 (October 22, 1913), 2. I am grateful to Laurie Stein of the Deutsche Werkbund Archiv for finding this article for me. There have been many important discussions of the Glass House. Two outstanding publications on its context within the Cologne exhibition are Kristina Hartmann and Franziska Bollerey, "Das Glashaus von Bruno Taut" (The glass house by Bruno Taut), in Thiekötter, ed., *Der westdeutsche Impuls*, 133; and Angelika Thiekötter, ed., *Kristallisationen, Splitterungen. Bruno Tauts Glashaus* (Crystallization, fragmentation: Bruno Taut's glass house) (Basel: Birkhäuser Verlag, 1993).

24. Paul Scheerbart, letter to Gottfried Heinersdorf, July 25, 1913, found in Rausch, ed., *70 Trillionen Weltgrüsse*, 457.

25. Ibid., n. 611.

26. There is considerable disagreement about the date on which Taut and Scheerbart met. Dennis Sharp writes that their relationship "goes back to the early days of . . . Der Sturm." This indicates a date closer to 1910. See *Glass Architecture by Paul Scheerbart and Alpine Architecture by Bruno Taut*, 10. Rosemarie Haag Bletter claims that "Taut had met Scheerbart in the circles of Der Sturm around 1912" in her essay "Paul Scheerbart's Architectural Fantasies," *Journal of the Society of Architectural Historians* 34 (May 1975), 96. On the other hand, Iain Boyd Whyte mentions that in 1912 Taut was an intimate of Herwarth Walden's Sturm circle, and that "Taut's first contact with Walden was made through the poet and fantasist Paul Scheerbart." See Iain Boyd Whyte, *Bruno Taut and the Architecture of Activism* (Cambridge: Cambridge University Press, 1982), 16.

27. Rausch, ed., *70 Trillionen Weltgrüsse*, 583 n. 613.

28. See Bruno Taut, "Glaserzeugung und Glasbau" (Glazing production and glass buildings), *Qualität* 1, no. 2 (April/May 1920), 9.

29. Bruno Taut, "Glasarchitektur," in *Die Glocke* (The bell) (March 8, 1921), 1376. This article also appeared in *Die Bauwelt* (Building world) 15, no. 10 (1921), 183–184.

30. Bruno Taut, *Alpine Architektur* (Vienna: Hagen, 1919). For images by Luckhardt, Scharoun, and other expressionist architects, see Wolfgang Pehnt, *Expressionist Architecture in Drawings* (New York: Van Nostrand Reinhold, 1985), 38, 48.

31. Adolf Behne, "Gedanken über Kunst und Zweck, dem Glashause gewid- met" (Thoughts on art and function, dedicated to the Glass House), *Kunst- gewerbeblatt* 27, no.1 (October 1915–1916), 1–4. The quotation is found on p. 4. Although Walter Benjamin picked up a secondhand copy of Scheerbart's novel in 1920, he never published comments about the work. See Walter Ben- jamin's letter to Gerhard Scholem, April 17, 1920, in Gershom Scholem and Theodor Adorno, eds., *The Correspondence of Walter Benjamin, 1910–1940* (Chicago: University of Chicago Press, 1994), 162.

32. Sigfried Giedion, *Walter Gropius: Work and Teamwork* (New York: Rein- hold, 1954), 46.

33. Ibid., 47. Giedion quotes the source as Bruno Taut, *Die neue Baukunst* (Stuttgart, 1929), 118.

34. Reyner Banham, "The Glass Paradise," in *A Critic Writes: Essays by Rey- ner Banham*, ed. Mary Banham (Berkeley: University of California Press, 1996), 34, 38.

35. Ibid., 34.

36. Bletter, "Scheerbart's Architectural Fantasies," 83–97. Bletter first pre- sented this research in her unpublished dissertation "Bruno Taut and Paul Scheerbart's Vision: Utopian Aspects of German Expressionist Architecture" (Ph.D. diss., Columbia University, 1973). Also see her excellent essay, "The In- terpretation of the Glass Dream: Expressionist Architecture and the History of

the Crystal Metaphor," *Journal of the Society of Architectural Historians* 40 (March 1981), 20–43.

37. Bletter, "Scheerbart's Architectural Fantasies," 96.

38. In a private conversation during the summer of 1997, Mechthild Rausch described her television show as being set in the Palm House in Berlin's Botanical Gardens, a site beloved by Scheerbart. In addition to the works by Rausch otherwise noted in the text, see Paul Scheerbart, *Jenseitsgalerie* (Gallery from beyond), ed. Mechthild Rausch (Munich: Klaus G. Renner, 1981). Rausch's most recent work on Scheerbart has been the publication of his "culture novelettes": Paul Scheerbart, *Der alte Orient. Kulturnovelletten aus Assyrien, Palmyra und Babylon* (The ancient Orient: Cultural novelettes from Assyria, Palmyra, and Babylon), ed. with an afterword by Mechthild Rausch (Munich: edition text + kritik, 1999). Rausch has compiled the most complete bibliography on Scheerbart to date. For the publication of Scheerbart's collected works, works about him, and his reception, see Paul Scheerbart, *Gesammelte Werke*, 10 vols. (Linkenheim: Edition Phantasia, 1986–1996).

39. A. H. Kober, "Das graue Tuch und zehn Prozent Weiß. Ein Damenroman. Von Paul Scheerbart," *Das literarische Echo* 19, no. 4 (1916–1917), 247–248. Kober's later writings seem to indicate a natural predilection toward Scheerbart's odd combination of religiosity and journalism. These include: A. H. Kober, *Geschichte der religiösen Dichtung in Deutschland. Ein Beitrag zur Entwicklungsgeschichte der deutsche Seele* (History of religious writing in Germany: A contribution to the developmental history of the German soul) (Essen: G. D. Baedeker, 1919); and *Die Seele des Journalisten; fünf Aufsätze zur Psychology der Presse* (The soul of the journalist: Five essays on the psychology of the press) (Cologne: Rheinland-Verlag, 1920).

40. Walther Petry, ed., *Humor der Nationen. Ausgewälte Prosa, Deutschland* (Humor of nations: Selected prose, Germany) (Berlin: Wertbuchhandel, 1925), 273–291.

41. Rausch's 1986 edition of *The Gray Cloth* elicited several contemporary reviews, which have been collected in Paul Kaltefleiter, ed., *Über Paul Scheerbart*

III. 100 Jahre Scheerbart-Rezeption; in drei Bänden (About Paul Scheerbart III: 100 years of Scheerbart's reception, in three volumes) (Paderborn: Igel Verlag, 1998). Thomas Anz writes in a review for the *Frankfurter Allgemeine Zeitung* (September 6, 1986): "'His style has the freshness of a child's cheek,' wrote Walter Benjamin in a fragment on Paul Scheerbart. He has scarcely lost any of his freshness over the past seventy years; childish innocence or naiveté were easily absent from this shrewd author from the start." See Kaltefleiter, *Über Paul Scheerbart III*, 247.

42. See D. C. Muecke, *The Compass of Irony* (London: Methuen, 1969), 182.

43. Peter Firchow, ed., *Friedrich Schlegel's* Lucinde *and the Fragments* (Minneapolis: University of Minnesota Press, 1971), 148.

44. See below, p. 3.

45. Scheerbart lists Swift first among earlier "inhabitants of Europe" to whom he feels he is "tied with a tighter thread." These also include François Rabelais, the German writer Heinrich Zschokke (1771–1848), and the German religious and social reformer Graf Nicholas Ludwig von Zinzendorf (1700–1760). He also claims that his artistic roots belong with the German romantics, particularly Brentano (1778–1842). This is best expressed in Scheerbart's brief autobiography compiled by Lubasch and Meyer, *Paul Scheerbart—Bibliographie mit einer Autobiographie.*

46. See below, pp. 102–103.

47. See Klaus-Jürgen Sembach, ed., *1910 Halbzeit der Moderne. Van de Velde, Behrens, Hoffmann und die Anderen* (Halftime of modernity: Van de Velde, Behrens, Hoffmann, and the others), exhibition catalogue (Stuttgart: Gerd Hatje, 1992), 35. See the depiction of the installation of a film projection in the large festival hall of the Paris exposition of 1900.

48. Reconstructions of real events using actors, sometimes referred to as "reconstitutions," were a common practice almost from the beginning of film production. See Erik Barnouw, *Documentary: A History of the Non-Fiction Film*

(London: Oxford University Press, 1974), 24–25; also Derek Paget, *No Other Way to Tell It: Dramadoc/Docudrama on Television* (Manchester: Manchester University Press, 1998).

49. See Stephen Kern, *The Culture of Time and Space* (Cambridge: Harvard University Press, 1983), 260.

50. See John E. Findling, *Chicago's Great World's Fairs* (Manchester: Manchester University Press, 1994), 26. Scheerbart foreshadowed several of the Viennese architect Joseph Urban's color and lighting innovations for the 1933 Century of Progress Exhibition in Chicago, including the extensive use of building illumination and searchlights. See ibid., 83–91. For more on the "White City," see David Burg, *Chicago's White City of 1893* (Lexington: University Press of Kentucky, 1976). For a discussion of the admiration of America ingenuity and invention in German-speaking countries around the turn of the century as well as the importance of the World's Columbian Exhibition, see Mitchell Schwarzer, *German Architectural Theory and the Search for Modern Identity* (Cambridge: Cambridge University Press, 1995), 143–144.

51. "But before the Hellenic civilization," Scheerbert writes, "there were already many colourful glass ampullae and lustrous majolica tiles in the countries bordering the Euphrates and Tigris, a thousand years before Christ. *The Near East is thus the so-called cradle of glass culture*" (emphasis mine). *Glass Architecture by Paul Scheerbart and Alpine Architecture by Bruno Taut*, 47.

52. Edward Said, *Orientalism* (New York: Random House, 1978), 19.

53. See below, p. 105.

54. Ibid., p. 41.

55. Said, *Orientalism*, 19.

56. For an overview of German aviation during this period, see Peter Fritzsche, *A Nation of Fliers: German Aviation and the Popular Imagination* (Cambridge: Harvard University Press, 1992). Transportation technology also figured

prominently in the German Werkbund at this time. See *Der Verkehr* (Transportation), an individual title of the *Jahrbuch des Deutschen Werkbundes* (Jena: E. Diederichs, 1914).

57. Quoted in Fritzsche, *A Nation of Fliers*, 11–12.

58. See below, p. 13.

59. The phrase is found in a letter dated December 19, 1912, to Herwarth Walden and is identified by Rausch as one of the working titles for *The Gray Cloth*. See *Rausch*, ed., *70 Trillionen Weltgrüsse*, 581 n. 601.

60. Scheerbart's allusion to *The Gray Cloth* as an "architects novel" is found in a letter dated March 18, 1913, to Hanns Ewers; his reference to it as "Müller's 'Ladies Novel'" appears in a missive to Bruno Taut of March 11, 1914. See Rausch, ed., *70 Trillionen Weltgrüsse*, 454, 468.

61. In private conversation, Mechthild Rausch suggested that the formula may refer to religious garments worn by Scheerbart's devout mother, who belonged to a strict Protestant sect whose members wore mostly gray clothing.

62. Paul Scheerbart, "Der Lichtklub von Batavia. Eine Damennovellette," *Die kritische Tribune* 1 (1912), 5–7.

63. Ibid., 6.

64. Ibid., 5–6.

65. In fact, the actions of the fictitious Mrs. Pline parallel Scheerbart's own attempts in July 1913 to found a Society for Glass Architects. See Rausch, ed., *70 Trillionen Weltgrüsse*, 455.

66. Rausch in her 1986 edition of Scheerbart, *Das graue Tuch*, 160.

67. Rausch, ed., *70 Trillionen Weltgrüsse*, 550 n. 411.

68. Anna's two pieces for *Die Frau und ihre Zeit* (1909) were "Der Stern in der Schürze. Ein Abend-Idyll" (The star in the apron: An evening idyll) and "Der Wundergarten" (The wonder garden). Rausch, ed., *70 Trillionen Weltgrüsse*, 568 n. 519. Her piece for the *Berliner Tageblatt* (apparently 1927, according to Rausch) was titled "Schlosser" (Locksmith) with the byline "nach Paul Scheerbart/von Anna Scheerbart" (after Paul Scheerbart/by Anna Scheerbart). Ibid., 550 n. 411. In a letter of September 24, 1909, to Franz Servaes, Paul Scheerbart expresses his "riesige Freude" (great joy) that Anna's two articles have been published (quoted in ibid., 393).

69. Gottfried Semper, *The Four Elements of Architecture and Other Writings*, trans. Harry Francis Mallgrave and Wolfgang Herrmann (Cambridge: Cambridge University Press, 1989), 254.

70. Quoted in Mark Wigley, "White Out: Fashioning the Modern," in Deborah Fausch, ed., *Architecture: In Fashion* (New York: Princeton Architectural Press, 1994), 186.

71. Adolf Loos, "Architecture" (1910), as quoted in Wigley, "White Out," 174.

72. Quoted in Sally Buchanan Kinsey, "A More Reasonable Way to Dress," in Wendy Kaplan, ed., *"The Art That Is Life": The Arts & Crafts Movement in America, 1875–1920* (Boston: Little, Brown, 1987), 364.

73. See below, p. 86.

74. See below, p. 77.

75. Adolf Behne, "Bruno Taut," in *Neue Blätter für Kunst und Dichtung* (New pages for art and poetry) 2 (April 1919–March 1920), 13–15.

76. See below, p. 80 (quoted in Behne, "Bruno Taut," 14).

77. Adolf Loos, "Ladies' Fashion," in *Spoken into the Void: Collected Essays 1897–1900* (Cambridge: MIT Press, 1982), 103.

78. Mary McLeod, "Undressing Architecture," in Fausch, ed., *Architecture: In Fashion*, 64.

79. Paul Scheerbart, *Das Paradies. Die Heimat der Kunst* (Berlin: George und Fiedler, 1889; rpt. Berlin: Verlag deutscher Phantasten, 1893).

80. Ibid., 163.

81. Ibid., 178.

82. Bruno Taut, "Architektur-Programm," December 1918, quoted in Whyte, *Bruno Taut and the Architecture of Activism*, 234.

83. Hendrik Petrus Berlage, "Architecture's Place in Modern Aesthetics" (1886), in *Thoughts on Style*, trans. Iain Boyd Whyte and Wim de Wit (Santa Monica: Getty Center Publication Programs, 1996), 102.

84. Gustav Theodor Fechner, *The Little Book of Life after Death*, trans. Mary C. Wadsworth (New York: Arno Press, 1977), 62–63. The work was first published in 1835. Fechner expressed his ideas most completely in volume 3 of his *Zend-Avesta, oder über die Dinge des Himmels und des Jenseits vom Standpunkt der Naturbetrachtung* (Zend-Avesta; or, On the things of heaven and the hereafter) (Leipzig: L. Voss, 1851).

85. In a letter of September 23, 1906, to the artist Alfred Kubin, Scheerbart explained how Fechner's theories helped him realize that "it was already quite common [to consider] the stars as really living beings." Rausch, ed., *70 Trillionen Weltgrüsse*, 322–325.

86. Paul Scheerbart, *Liwûna und Kaidôh. Ein Seelenroman* (Leipzig: Inselverlag, 1902).

87. The design fantasies described by Scheerbart in *Liwûna and Kaidôh* show similarities to the building for the Point Loma Theosophical Society. This project was constructed between 1896 and 1901 outside of San Diego under the leadership of Katherine Tingley. It included chairs of swirling organic forms

created by Reginald Machell and colored-glass domes. A religious movement founded by Helena P. Blavatsky in 1875, theosophy shared with Fechner's psychophysics notions of universal divinity and the reincarnation of the soul. Scheerbart mentions it in *Glasarchitektur.* See Bruce Kamerling, "The Arts and Crafts Movement in San Diego," in Kenneth R. Trapp, ed., *The Arts and Crafts Movement in California: Living the Good Life* (Oakland: Abbeville Press, 1993), 208–211.

88. Paul Scheerbart, *Lesabéndio. Ein Asteroiden-Roman,* with fourteen illustrations by Alfred Kubin (Munich and Berlin: Georg Müller, 1913). Scheerbart appears to have started work on *Lesabéndio* around 1906, when it had the working title of "Lesabéndio, the Sad King." See Scheerbart's letter to Erich Mühsam of March 19, 1906, in Rausch, ed., *70 Trillionen Weltgrüsse,* 306. For Müller's selection of Kubin as illustrator, see Rausch, ed., *70 Trillionen Weltgrüsse,* 579 n. 584.

89. See Scholem and Adorno, eds., *Correspondence of Walter Benjamin,* 153 n. 2, 155 n. 2.

90. Paul Scheerbart, *Lesabéndio,* as reprinted in Paul Scheerbart, *Gesammelte Werke,* vol. 5 (Linkenheim: Edition Phantasia, 1988), 294.

91. Paul Scheerbart, *Die Entwicklung des Luftmilitarismus,* as translated in Kern, *The Culture of Time and Space,* 243.

92. Rausch, *Von Danzig ins Weltall,* 67.

93. It should be noted that Scheerbart also contributed regularly to several contemporary journals including *Die Gegenwart* (The Present), *Das Theater, Die Aktion,* and *Der Sturm* (The Assault), as well as many newspapers.

94. See chapter 10, "Lokalreporter beim *Danziger Courier*" (Local reporter for the *Danzig Courier*), in Rausch, *Von Danzig ins Weltall,* 91–101.

95. See Peter Fritzsche, *Reading Berlin 1900* (Cambridge: Harvard University Press, 1996), 2.

96. Ibid., 44, 106.

97. Paul Scheerbart, "Das Panorama der Hohenzollern-Galerie" (The panorama of the Hohenzollern Gallery), *Das Atelier* 2, no. 30 (1891–1892), 8; Paul Scheerbart, "Das ägyptische Museum zu Berlin" (The Egyptian Museum in Berlin), *Das Atelier* 2, no. 35 (1891–1892), 4–5; Paul Scheerbart, "Die Polychromie in der Frontarchitektur" (Polychromy in facade architecture), *Das Atelier* 1, no. 7 (1890–1891), 5–7.

98. Paul Scheerbart, "Berlins architektonische Plastik," in *Berliner Pflaster. Illustrierte Schilderungen aus dem Berliner Leben* (Berlin's pavement: Illustrated descriptions from life in Berlin) (Berlin: M. Reymond & L. Manzel, 1893), 60–65.

99. Paul Scheerbart, "Der Architektenkongress. Eine Parlamentsgeschichte," *Berliner Tageblatt,* June 1913, reprinted in *Frühlicht* 1 (Fall 1921), 26–27.

100. Ibid., 26.

101. Ibid., 27.

102. Le Corbusier, *Towards a New Architecture* (New York: Dover Publications, 1986), 11.

103. Editors' preface to Scheerbart, "Das Glashaus. Ein Vorbericht," 2.

104. Paul Scheerbart, "Glashäuser. Bruno Tauts Glaspalast auf der Werkbund-Ausstellung in Cöln" (Glass houses: Bruno Taut's glass palace at the Werkbund Exhibition in Cologne), *Technische Monatshefte* (Technical Monthly) 4, no. 8 (1914), 106–107.

105. Walter Benjamin, "The Storyteller," in Benjamin, *Illuminations*, ed. Hannah Arendt, trans. Harry Zohn (New York: Schocken Books, 1969), 99.

SELECTED
BIBLIOGRAPHY

This chronological selection lists individual editions of Scheerbart's book-length works. Although most appeared during the author's lifetime, several shorter stories and translations were published after his death. This bibliography is the first to provide English-speaking audiences with access to the breadth of Scheerbart's literary contributions. The most complete bibliography of Scheerbart's work accompanies Mechthild Rausch's 1999 edition of *Der alte Orient. Kulturnovelletten aus Assyrien, Palmyra und Babylon,* listed below.

Das Paradies. Die Heimat der Kunst (Paradise: Homeland of art). Berlin: Commissions-Verlag von George und Fiedler, 1889. Reprint, Berlin: Verlag deutscher Phantasten, 1893.

Ja . . . was . . . möchten wir nicht Alles! Ein Wunderfabelbuch (Yes . . . what . . . would we not like everything! A book of miraculous fables). Berlin: Verlag deutscher Phantasten, 1893. Reprint, edited and with an afterword by Susanne Bek and Michael Schardt and with illustrations by Claudia Neuhaus, Paderhorn: Igel, 1992.

Tarub, Bagdads berühmte Köchin. Arabischer Kulturroman (Tarub, Baghdad's famous [female] cook: Arabian culture novel). Berlin: Verein für deutsches Schrifthum, 1897. Reprint, Minden: J. C. C. Bruns, 1900. Reprint, edited and with an afterword by Matthias Schardt, Paderhorn: Igel, 1992. Translated into Dutch by R. C. van H., Nijmegen: E. & M. Cohen, 1898.

Ich liebe Dich! Ein Eisenbahnroman mit 66 Intermezzos (I love you! A railroad novel with sixty-six intermezzos). Berlin: Schuster und Loeffler, 1897. Reprint, edited and with an afterword by Matthias Schardt, Siegen: Affholderbach und Strohmann, 1987.

Der Tod der Barmekiden. Arabischer Haremsroman (Death of Barmekiden: Arabian harem novel). Leipzig: Kriesende Ringe–Max Spohr, 1897.

Na Prost! Phantastischer Königsroman (Cheers! Fantastic King's Novel). Berlin: Schuster und Loeffler, 1898. Reprint, edited and with an afterword by Matthias Schardt, Siegen: Affholderbach und Strohmann, 1987.

Rakkóx der Billionär. Ein Protzenroman. Die wilde Jagd. Ein Entwicklungsroman (Rakkóx the Billionaire: A snobs novel. The wild hunt: An evolution novel). With a drawing by Felix Valloton and book ornamentation by Henri Jossot. Leipzig: Insel, 1900. Reprint, with an afterword by Franz Rottensteiner, Frankfurt am Main: Insel, 1976. Reprint, Munich: Klaus G. Renner, 1982. Translated into Czech by Karel Kamínek, Prague: Otto, 1908.

Selected Bibliography

Die Seeschlange. Ein See-Roman (The sea-serpent: A sea novel). Minden: J. C. C. Bruns, 1901.

Liwûna und Kaidôh. Ein Seelenroman (Liwûna and Kaidôh: A souls novel). Leipzig: Inselverlag, 1902.

Die große Revolution. Ein Mondroman (The great revolution: A moon novel). Leipzig: Insel, 1902.

Immer mutig! Ein phantastischer Nilpferderoman (Always daring! A fantastic hippopotamus novel). With book ornamentation by Paul Scheerbart. Minden: J. C. C. Bruns, 1902. Reprint, Frankfurt am Main: Suhrkamp Taschenbuch, 1990.

Der Aufgang zur Sonne. Hausmärchen (The ascent to the sun: House fairy-tale). With a cover drawing by Paul Scheerbart. Minden: J. C. C. Bruns, 1903. Reprint, with illustrations by Horst Hussel, Leipzig and Weimar: Gustav Kiepenheuer, 1984.

Kometentanz. Australe Pantomime in 2 Aufzügen (Comet dance: Astral pantomime in two acts). With book ornamentation by Paul Scheerbart. Leipzig: Insel, 1903.

Cervantes. Berlin: Schuster und Loeffler, 1904. Reprint, Erlangen: K. G. Renner, 1979.

Revolutionäre Theater-Bibliothek (Revolutionary Theater Library). With book decoration and illustrations by Paul Scheerbart. Berlin: Eduard Eisselt, 1904.

Der Kaiser von Utopia. Ein Volksroman (The emperor of utopia: A people's novel). With book ornamentation by Paul Scheerbart. Berlin: Eduard Eisselt, 1904.

Münchhausen und Clarissa. Ein Berliner Roman (Münchhausen and Clarissa: A Berlin novel). With book ornamentation by Paul Scheerbart. Berlin: Oesterheld & Co., 1906.

Selected Bibliography

Jenseitsgalerie. Ein Mappenwerk. (Gallery from beyond: A portfolio). Berlin: Oesterheld & Co., 1907.

Flora Mohr. Eine Glasblumen-Novellette in 8 Kapiteln (Flora Mohr: A glass-flower novelette in eight chapters). Prague: Haase, 1909.

Kater-Poesie (Tomcat poetry). Berlin and Leipzig: Ernst Rowohlt, 1909. Reprint, Berlin: Ernst Rowohlt, 1920.

Die Entwicklung des Luftmilitarismus und die Auflösung der europäischen Land-Heere, Festungen und Seeflotten. Eine Flugschrift (The development of air militarism and the dissolution of European land armies, fortifications, and navies: A pamphlet). Berlin: Oesterheld & Co., 1909.

Das Perpetuum mobile. Die Geschichte einer Erfindung (The perpetual motion machine: The story of an invention). Leipzig: Ernst Rowohlt, 1910. Reprint, with illustrations by Dieter Roth, Erlangen: Klaus G. Renner, 1977. Reprint, with illustrations by Johannes Vennekamp, Munich and Salzburg: Klaus G. Renner, 1997.

Das große Licht. Ein Münchhausen-Brevier (The big light: A Münchhausen breviary). Leipzig: Sally Rabinowitz, 1912.

Astrale Novelletten (Astral novelettes). Karlsruhe and Leipzig: Dreililien, 1912. Reprint, Munich and Leipzig: Georg Müller, 1912. Reprint, with introduction by Richard Elchinger, Munich: Die Weltliteratur, 1919.

Lesabéndio. Ein Asteroïden-Roman (Lesabéndio: An asteroid novel). With illustrations by Alfred Kubin. Munich and Leipzig: Georg Müller, 1913. Reprint, with an afterword by Paul Raabe, Munich: Deutscher Taschenbuch Verlag, 1964. Reprint, with an afterword by Kai Pfankuch, Hofheim: Wolke, 1986. Reprint, Frankfurt am Main: Suhrkamp Taschenbuch, 1986. Translated into Italian by Piera di Segni and Fabrizio Desideri, Rome: Editori Riuniti, 1982.

Das graue Tuch und zehn Prozent Weiß. Ein Damenroman (The gray cloth and ten percent white: A ladies novel). Munich and Leipzig: Georg Müller, 1914.

Selected Bibliography

Reprint, with an afterword by Mechthild Rausch, Munich: edition text + kritik, 1986.

Glasarchitektur (Glass architecture). Berlin: Verlag Der Sturm, 1914. Reprint, with an afterword by Wolfgang Pehnt, Munich: Rogner und Bernhard, 1971. Reprint, with an afterword by Mechthild Rausch, Berlin: Gebr. Mann Verlag, 2000. Compiled (with Bruno Taut's *Alpine Architecture*) by Dennis Sharp and translated into English by James Palmes, New York: Praeger, 1972. Translated into Italian by Mario Fabbri and with an afterword by Giulio Schiavoni, Milan: Adelphi, 1982.

Die Mopsiade. Berlin: Alfred Richard Meyer, 1920.

Das Lachen ist verboten . . . (Laughter is forbidden . . .). Berlin: See-Igel-Verlag Fritz Nürnberger, 1929.

Machtspäße. Arabische Novelletten (Antics of Power: Arabian novelettes). With book ornamentation by Paul Scheerbart. Munich: Klaus G. Renner, 1981.

Lifakûbo iba solla . . . With etchings by Horst Hussel. Berlin: Berlinische Galerie/Horst Hussel, 1993.

Sonntagsplauderei (Sunday chats). With etchings by Horst Hussel. Berlin: Dronte Presse, 1994.

Wenn Knaben fromm sind. Eine Knabengeschichte (When boys are pious: A boys story). With etchings by Horst Hussel. Berlin: Dronte Presse, 1995.

Luftschlösser. Eine peruanische Geschichte (Air palaces: A Peruvian story). With etchings by Horst Hussel. Berlin: Dronte Presse, 1996.

Der alte Orient. Kulturnovelletten aus Assyrien, Palmyra und Babylon (The ancient Orient: Culture novelettes from Assyria, Palmyra, and Babylon). Edited and with an afterword by Mechthild Rausch. Munich: edition text + kritik, 1999.